A Very British Lord
By
G.L. Snodgrass

Purple Herb Publishing

Email - GL@glsnodgrass.com

http://glsnodgrass.com/

Amazon Author Page

https://www.bookbub.com/authors/g-l-snodgrass

https://www.facebook.com/G.L.Snodgrass/

Return to your favorite ebook retailer or the blog linked above to discover other works by G.L. Snodgrass. Thank you for your support.

A Very British Lord

Dedicated To

Kim Strong

A Very British Lord

Chapter One

Miss Isobel Stafford looked into her nephew's eyes and sighed with contentment.

There was something about holding an infant that filled her soul. It made her heart ache with pure happiness. This was what the world was about, she thought with a bit of surprise.

The way his blue eyes searched hers, filled with curiosity and trust. The way he smelled of fresh life, full of potential. New, glorious. It was enough to make a woman swoon with need.

She smiled at his tiny hand grasping her finger. Each of his little fingers so perfectly sculpted. Even his starched lace christening gown pulled at her heart.

And this one is special, she thought. Besides being his aunt, she was to be his Godmother. A privileged responsibility Lydia and Cambridge had given her. Even if it did mean sharing the honor with that man.

Isobel pushed aside the annoyance. The least Lydia could have done was chose someone different to be the godfather. But no. The Duke of Cambridge had insisted on Lord Brookenham, and Lydia had refused to disagree with her husband. It was amazing what a woman would put up with for the man she loved.

Glancing over at her nemesis from beneath her brow, she had to stop herself from frowning. The man was too large and too handsome. And things always seemed to go his way. It made her grit her teeth for some reason. As if his mere existence was something she had to tolerate.

He caught her looking at him and smirked. The same smirk she had seen for the last five years. That look that said he knew better. That she was nothing but a little girl and would never understand the truths about life. It was the same smirk he had given her on their first meeting when she was but fourteen years of age. He an Earl, she and her sisters nothing more than common girls living off his uncle's charity.

The smirk that sent an angry spike to her shoulders.

Even now, her Aunt Ester continued to live in the same leaky cottage on his estate. No matter how hard the three of them had tried, Aunt Ester had refused to move to London. Saying she preferred to live the quiet country life in Wycombe.

The fact that her family continued to benefit from his charity was galling, to say the least. Especially considering the wealth of both Norwich and Cambridge. It could all be solved if Aunt Ester would simply come to London.

Isobel shuddered to think of being away from London. The museums, the parties. No, her

Aunt Ester didn't understand what she was missing.

Biting the inside of her lip, she returned her focus on the baby as the Bishop said the words welcoming the child into the church.

Of course, holding little Thomas brought to life all the regrets and doubts that had been bothering her. Especially lately. Reminding her once again that her life was racing by without her.

This was the start of her third season and she was still alone. At almost twenty, and with two Dukes for brothers-in-law. It wasn't right. The world was open before her. She had every opportunity. But no, she had failed to find the right match. A fact that The Dowager Duchess of Norwich was not remiss in reminding her of almost daily.

Why was it so hard to find what her sisters had found?

Looking over at them she held back a cringe of jealousy. Both Ann and Lydia had found strong men they loved and that loved them. Both had families. Both had purpose. Why couldn't she find that?

What was she lacking that held her back from finding that happiness? Why had the men she met seem so ... lacking? There could be no better word for it. They seemed dull and uncurious. Or worse, arrogant and hopeless.

No, it wasn't her, she thought. It was them. Of course, a girl could only tell herself that so often before she began to doubt herself.

As the Bishop's words echoed in the large cathedral, Thomas' older brother Johnathon fidgeted next to Lydia. His father beside him, smiling at the baby in her arms.

Johnathan's hand was buried in the folds of his mother's dress, looking as if he were overwhelmed. All of these people and they were all focused on his new baby brother. He must feel so left out, she thought. She must make a point of doing something special with him later. A two-year-old needed love from his aunt just as much as a new baby.

Looking once again into the crystal clear blue eyes of the baby in her arms, her heart melted. Family. That was what was important. Nothing more so. A new determination filled her. She would find someone this year.

She would focus and be more honest with herself. Perhaps she was not destined to find her true love. Perhaps she must realize that she would never find the same happiness her sisters had found.

But a family would go a long way to filling that emptiness inside of her. Of that, she was most assured.

.o0o.

The Earl of Brookenham fought to hold back a yawn as the Bishop droned on. It wouldn't be right to be disrespectful in church. People didn't like that sort of thing. And word would get back to his mother. It always seemed to.

But it had been a late night, a common occurrence of late.

But what was a man to do? His best friends were married, settled down with children. He, however, was most definitely not married, and he hoped never to be. Thankfully, he had two critical assets that would assist him in that matter. Two cousins, both with sons. There were more than enough qualified men to assume the title when the time came.

No. There was no need for him ever to be trapped by marriage.

Looking over at his friend Cambridge and the way he looked at his son. A sharp pain of regret flashed through him. He would not know that feeling of pride and contentment, he realized. Never know what it felt like to be a father.

But that was a price he was willing to pay if it meant avoiding the hell known as matrimony.

He was a wealthy, powerful young man. A British Lord. Why would he ever wish to tie himself to one woman? The thought seemed preposterous. Of course, many men of his status chose to continue their wild escapades even after marriage.

But he refused to commit to vows that he intended on breaking. Although, he thought with regret, a bad marriage might result in a man taking a mistress. He might have no other choice.

Shaking off a shudder at the thought of being married, he glanced over at Isobel and had to hold back a smile. The girl had grown up to be a beautiful woman. Of that, there was no doubt.

The sparkling green eyes combined with her auburn hair was tantalizing. Especially when added to a figure designed by the gods to tempt a man, and a face sculpted by a master craftsman to capture the best of the feminine.

Of course, when added to the generous dowry, she drew the wrong type of man. As evidenced by the surrounding pack of jackals he saw her with at most events. The men seemed to be a combination of idiots, fortune hunters, and ne'er do wells. Thankfully, it was Norwich and Cambridge's problem, not his.

One thing he had learned long ago, not to interact with the young Miss Stafford, unless absolutely necessary. The girl's tongue was as sharp as a fencing foil.

You would think that being an Earl might offer some protection. But the girl had never viewed it that way. Sometimes he thought she took particular pleasure in pointing out his failings. Whether it was his dancing ability. Or his conversational capability. His choice of dress or the company he kept.

There was no subject out of bounds when it came to Miss Isobel.

The worse though, was when she pointed out his reputation. It seemed she did not approve of his late-night activities.

Although, how a mere slip of a girl ever found out about such things he would never know. What he did know though was that she never hesitated in pointing them out.

It was only because of his friendship with Norwich and Cambridge that he even tolerated her sharp tongue. If not for them, he would have been able to avoid her entirely. They would have been nothing more than distant acquaintances.

But this was the high society of Britain, and everyone knew everyone. The same parties. And like today. Being asked to be Godfather to little Thomas. Some things could not be avoided.

She did look good though, he thought as a sense of male appreciation passed through him. She had always looked particularly beautiful. But here, standing with the baby in her arms. There was something that pulled at him.

She would be a good mother he realized. Intelligent, caring. But most of all, fiercely protective. A lioness with her cubs. The thought made him smile. He pitied the person who ever tried to stop Miss Isobel Stafford. They would fail every time.

.oOo.

Isobel felt a sharp pang of regret as she handed little Thomas back to his mother. An emptiness filled her as she watched Lydia tuck the blanket around the baby and coo sweet motherly words as she rubbed her cheek next to his.

Holding off a tear that threatened the corner of her eye, she glanced up to find Lord Brookenham looking at her with a strange expression.

What was that all about? she wondered. The two of them had an unofficial agreement not to interact. It was best for their friends and family. Over the years they had mutually learned which subjects to avoid. Politics, religion, and art, topping the list. But she was rather positive, if they tried, they could find a dozen more.

No, they limited themselves to talking about the weather, friends, and family, and … That was it, she realized. The only safe subjects.

A disappointment flashed through her. It was a shame, the man was intelligent. He had won too many arguments too easily not to be. He was well read. It would have been nice to conduct in-depth discussions with him.

But they always seemed to become heated too quickly. Lydia called it lamp oil and fire. Two things that could not be brought together without an explosion.

Isobel sighed as she turned to focus on her family. Gray Wolf, Cambridge's native Indian friend stood aside, watching the ceremony with detached curiosity. Norwich and Ann were congratulating the parents. The Dowager smiled, obviously pleased that things had gone without a hitch. The woman despised public embarrassments.

Taking the toddler, Johnathan's little hand, she pulled him to the side and scrunched down to give him a quick hug. The small boy wrapped his hands around her neck and pulled tightly.

Yes, she thought, family.

Perhaps someday her own child would hug her this   way.

Chapter Two

Lord Brookenham looked out over the crowd and sighed. Why was he even here? Another party. Another ball given by an old biddy who wanted him to marry her daughter.

No, he thought. His mother might push. Society might expect him to give up his freedom. But no. It wasn't going to happen. There were too many widows and fallen women to enjoy.

Sighing again, he turned away so that he could find a back room and perhaps talk some young idiot in joining him at the gambling tables. If he was lucky, he might be able to save the evening after all.

"Brookenham," a voice called to him as he entered the parlor.

The young Earl smiled. Norwich had already established a table in the far corner. His friend smiled and waved him over. Brookenham wove his way through the other tables. Reminding himself not to play for high stakes with Norwich at the table. The man was too good. No, his targets must be easier quarry.

"If you will excuse me, gentleman," Norwich said to the other men at the table. "I must discuss a matter with Brookenham here."

The three other men frowned, obviously upset with the idea of Norwich leaving before they had an opportunity to win their money back.

Brookenham could only smile. They were lucky they had any money left at all. In fact, perhaps he should return to this table after he had dealt with Norwich. Both Baron Handfield and Lord Dorchester were well off. Yes, he would return.

He didn't need the money. No, it was the sport, the contest he loved. Besting another man with intellect and skill. Could there be any better accomplishment? Perhaps the boxing ring, but that wasn't available at the moment.

"Do you have a moment Brookenham?" Norwich asked as he indicated they should step out into the garden for a bit of privacy.

Lord Brookenham raised an eyebrow as a nervousness tickled his stomach. It was unusual for the Duke of Norwich to ask anything of him. Normally it was the other way around. The Duke had been his mentor and friend ever since a Frenchman's bullet had taken Brookenham's older brother Johnathon in Portugal.

The Duke had been more than a brother. More than a father even. Kind, at times disproving. But always willing to help. Brookenham would do anything for the man. Heaven knew he owed him much. But it was more than that. Norwich just set the example of the man he hoped to be. The thought of saying no to any request was preposterous.

As they stepped outside, Norwich took a deep breath and frowned. Brookenham waited, surprised in the hesitancy in his friend. It must be serious.

"I have a favor to request ..." the Duke began after he had gathered himself.

"Of course," Brookenham answered before the Duke could finish.

His Grace frowned at him and shook his head. "You haven't even heard the request. I do not think you will be so willing once you do."

Brookenham's stomach clenched into a tight ball. This couldn't be good.

"Ann is increasing," Norwich said with a frown showing his obvious concern about his wife's health.

"Congratulations," Brookenham answered, happy for his friend. He well knew how much they wanted another child.

Norwich nodded but continued to frown. "The Doctors are worried. She had such difficulty last time. I must say that I share their concern."

Brookenham frowned, Ann, the Duchess of Norwich was one of his favorite people. Open, happy, never judgmental. Everyone loved her. Unlike her younger sister Isobel, he thought.

"Is there anything I can do?" he asked the Duke.

Norwich took a deep breath. "As you know, Cambridge and Lydia have already returned to

Stonewall with the baby. Getting him back here to London will be impossible."

Brookenham laughed, the Duke's comment had barely scratched the surface. The Duke of Cambridge hated London with a passion. Suddenly, his stomach tightened up even more as he took a deep breath and held it, waiting for the Duke to continue.

"I have discussed it with both Prinny and Liverpool. They have accepted that I will be returning to my estate with my wife. I know her. She will not rest unless I am there to force her."

Brookenham nodded as he tried to understand why this was significant. Granted, he would have preferred for Norwich to remain in London. He enjoyed his company. But, it wasn't as if their paths would not cross. England was not that big. Their Estates were only two days from London and two days from each other.

"And," Norwich continued, "as you know, this is young Isobel's third season. There have already been comments. If she does not find a husband soon she will be put on the shelf and passed over."

Brookenham gasped, surely the Duke was not going to ask him to take the woman as a bride. He would do anything for the man, but surely he would not ask that of him. No man should ever be asked to make such a sacrifice.

Norwich saw the look on his face and laughed as he shook his head. "No, not that my friend."

The young Earl let out a long breath as a cold chill passed down his spine as if he had dodged certain death.

"No," the Duke continued, "but because this might be Isobel's last opportunity. We have decided to let her remain here in London with my mother. Perhaps both of them working together might find her a husband."

Brookenham nodded. It made sense. Although why she was having any problem was a complete mystery. There were more than a dozen men, each more than appropriate who would be willing to take the woman as a bride.

But of course, Isobel refused to make a decision. He remembered overhearing Ann mention once that Isobel's problem was that she continually thought she could do better. A fact that just confirmed his opinion about the girl. She saw herself as something special. As deserving more.

A remarkable attitude when you considered her young life growing up in a ramshackle country cottage. A commoner with no family of significance. At least, not at that time. Not until her sister had married the Duke of Norwich. And yet, she dismissed Lords and wealthy men as not being up to her standards.

The concept was completely foreign. Every other woman he knew would have looked out over the field and simply picked the best candidate. The wealthiest, highest title. What more could she want? Her beauty, family connections, and large dowry would ensure she was rewarded with her choice.

But not Isobel Stafford. No, for her, it must be the best. Unfortunately, for her, the best meant unique, unusual, different.

"So, both Cambridge and yourself will be absent," Brookenham said to his friend as he frowned, wondering what the man might want.

Norwich sighed again, "Yes, Well," he said. "I am concerned, leaving Isobel alone with our crowd. You know how it is. She has a habit of attracting the worst."

Brookenham laughed, that was saying it lightly. Then a sudden panic filled him as he realized what his friend was going to ask of him.

"You wish me to keep an eye on things," he said as a sick feeling of dread filled him.

Norwich nodded. "I wouldn't ask this, but Ann feels it is vital that Isobel remain here in London. And I am concerned that if I make an issue of it, Ann might refuse to return to our estate."

Brookenham nodded absently as he pondered the situation. Keeping an eye on Isobel might be a difficult task. The woman had a rebellious streak a mile wide. If she thought he of all people was interfering, she was likely to make a poor choice just to prove him wrong.

"Do you plan on informing her that you asked me to watch over her?"

The Duke snorted and quickly shook his head at the stupidity of the idea. Brookenham could only laugh.

"No, I don't think that will be necessary," the Duke said. "All you need to do is keep an eye out. Ensure she is not taken advantage of. Keep her from being compromised. Isobel is an intelligent woman. She can take care of herself. Or at least she thinks she can. No, I need you to be enough of a presence to remind the cads and rakes to take care."

Brookenham nodded. A task that he was more than qualified to handle. Whether it was the boxing ring, or if necessary, the dueling fields. His reputation would make most men hesitate.

"Of course," the Duke continued, "if you become aware of a potential issue, you must send word right away and I will deal with it."

The Earl laughed, "You don't get to keep all the fun to yourself, my friend. If I am going to do this, I must be allowed to follow through."

Norwich thought for a moment then nodded. "Of course. But still, I would expect word. You should also inform Cambridge. Between the three of us, we should be able to handle any problem that might occur."

They both looked at each other. Both of them very aware that when it came to Isobel Stafford. There was every possibility that something might occur.

Sighing to himself, Brookenham grimaced as he nodded. It was settled then. Miss Isobel Stafford would be his charge this season. At least until either of her sisters or brothers-in-law returned to town. Suddenly, a deep worry filled him. This was not going to go well, he realized.

.oOo.

Isobel curtsied to Lord Dorchester as he bowed at the waist. The two of them smiled at each other as he held out an arm to escort her back to The Dowager.

The older woman watched them like a hawk as they made their way through the crowd. She needn't have worried. Lord Dorchester was married with three children. What was more, his wife was a good friend.

But The Dowager always looked like that. As if men were naturally on the hunt to take advantage of a young woman.

Not all men were like that, Isobel knew. But The Dowager would never change.

Lord Dorchester bowed to The Dowager, thanked Isobel once again for the dance then turned and left them alone.

The Dowager frowned at his back then glanced at Isobel and shook her head.

"What?" Isobel asked as she quickly ran a hand over her dress to make sure everything was in place.

"You should not be wasting your time dancing with married men."

Isobel flicked her fan open to hide the roll of her eyes.

"I am serious Isobel, you need to focus."

"Your Grace," Isobel said, "I am not going to find the right husband because I danced with him. It doesn't work that way."

The Dowager scoffed as she turned to look out over the crowd. Obviously searching for another target.

Isobel sighed inside. Why was it so difficult? Why couldn't she simply meet the man of her dreams and both of them fall in love then build a life together?

A movement across the room caught her eye. Height, wavy brown hair, wide shoulders.

"What is he doing here?" Isobel hissed as she brought her fan up, hoping to hide behind it. Hoping somehow that Lord Brookenham would not become aware of her presence.

The Dowager frowned as she shrugged. "Why wouldn't he be? Lady Eddington is well respected. Everyone who is anyone is here."

Isobel shot a quick glance towards Lord Brookenham and shook her head. The man kept appearing at the worst time. She was due to dance with Lord Darlington next. The Viscount had made a point of finding her early and gaining a place on her dance card. A waltz no less.

For some reason, she was disturbed by the idea of Brookenham watching her while she danced a waltz with one of the most handsome Lords in Britain. The fact that Darlington's reputation was less than stellar only added to the sense of danger."

No sooner had the thought occurred to her than Viscount Darlington broke through the crowd and approached her. His fine blond hair, deep blue eyes, and handsome face were what drove the whispers of the young women of the ton.

"Your Grace, Miss Stafford," the Viscount said as he bowed over her hand. "I believe this is my dance."

The Dowager frowned at her. Isobel bit her tongue, she hadn't told The Dowager that she had agreed to a waltz with Lord Darlington. A fact that The Dowager's look told her they would discuss later.

Smiling to the man across from her, she allowed him to lead her out to the dance floor. As the music started, the Viscount's arms slid into place and they began to twirl. A small flutter touched her stomach.

The man was handsome, of that there was no doubt. And more than one woman was looking at them with jealousy, more than enough reason to make a woman feel special in his arms.

What kind of husband would the man make? she wondered as he expertly maneuvered them around the dance floor. A stupid question, she thought to herself. She had only met the man earlier in the evening when Lady Eddington had introduced them.

He danced well, she thought. That was something. A husband should be able to dance. But what else did she know about the man?

He had a small estate in the Lake district. His family was not particularly well connected. He was liberal in his politics, like most of the lords, a supporter of Prinny.

It was his reputation though that she was curious about. She had heard the rumors. Something about a young woman who had found herself rejected no doubt. Surely a British Lord would not be dishonorable. No, it was probably a false story.

"I must say, Miss Stafford," Lord Darlington said as he looked down into her eyes. "You dance divinely."

"You act surprised, My Lord."

He laughed and realized she liked his laugh. A wife should like her husband's laugh she thought.

"Not at all, Miss Stafford. I assure you."

Isobel smiled up at him until she felt his arm pull her a little closer. Suddenly a worry filled her. If people saw them dancing too closely, there would be talk. And despite having a powerful brother-in-law, a young woman couldn't survive the wrong type of gossip.

Luckily, the dance came to an end. Lord Darlington bent over her hand, his lips barely touching the back of her glove, sending a faint tingle up her arm.

He rose and held her stare for a moment. She swallowed hard then slipped her arm into his so that he could lead her back to The Dowager.

"Perhaps another dance later," he said before they could break through the crowd around them.

Isobel's heart fluttered for a moment, he liked her she realized. A man didn't ask for another dance unless he was interested in pursuing things further.

As they turned the corner, her stomach fell when she saw Lord Brookenham standing next to The Dowager shooting her a glare that could melt a mountain of ore.

Why was he so upset? she wondered. They hadn't even talked and he was already mad at her.

Swallowing hard, she tried to push away the feeling that she had done something wrong. She had simply danced with a man. And what gave Brookenham any right to frown at her as if she had run away with a footman.

"Darlington," the Earl said with a strong frown as he glared at the Viscount.

"Brookenham," the man next to her said, returning the frown.

Isobel looked first at one and then at the other as the two men held each other's stare, neither willing to back down.

What was this? Isobel wondered. Since when did Brookenham care who she danced with. It was not like he ever asked her himself. Why were these two acting like tomcats in a back alley?

"How is your mother, Brookenham?" The Dowager asked, forcing him to look at her and away from Lord Darlington.

"She is doing well, Your Grace," he said as he returned to staring at Darlington.

After a few more beats, Lord Darlington turned to Isobel and said, "Thank you, Miss Stafford. I do look forward to dancing with you again."

Lord Brookenham snorted.

Isobel shot him an angry look then quickly returned to Lord Darlington and smiled her best smile and curtsied briefly. She was looking forward to learning more about this man. In fact, she wanted to learn quite a bit.

Once he was gone, Lord Brookenham frowned at her.

Why was he so upset? Isobel wondered. She had finally gotten out from under the ever watchful eye of His Grace. And now, here was Lord Brookenham acting as if she was his ward. When the Duke and Ann had left, Isobel had felt as if a heavy weight had been lifted from her shoulders. She had expected them to change their minds at the last minute. She had never thought they would leave her alone here in London.

But now, she was once again having to second guess every move. Between The Dowager and Lord Brookenham, her life was as confined as when Ann watched over her every move.

A sudden thought flew into her awareness. My God, Norwich had asked his friend to watch over her.

No, this could not be allowed. How dare they. Him, of all people. No.

Gritting her teeth, she forced herself to smile up at the tall Earl. No, she was not going to be treated like a child. Especially not by this man.

Chapter Three

Isobel examined the plain cotton dress and smiled.

"This will be perfect," she said to her maid, Maggie. It was the type of dress a maid would wear on her day off. Or perhaps a seamstress. The kind of dress that would allow her to blend in.

Her maid frowned as she shook her head. "This is not wise, Miss," the young maid said. "If Her Grace ever finds out, she … I don't know what will happen.

Isobel laughed as she began to undress so that she could don the disguise. "Don't worry, they are in Kent. She will never learn. Neither will His Grace. Besides, it is only an afternoon at the museum."

The maid rolled her eyes as she helped Isobel out of her dress and into the simpler garment. Isobel could only smile. It would be nice to blend in with the other people for a change. To disappear into anonymity.

Combining the dress with a common bonnet would do the trick, she was sure of it.

"I must say, this is not the way a proper Lady should act," Maggie said as she shook her head. "Sneaking out, traveling about London without an escort. It just isn't done."

Isobel laughed. "Don't forget, I am not a Lady …"

"If you don't act accordingly, you never will be," Maggie said as she pulled at her mistress' dress to make sure it fell correctly.

"You will love the museum," Isobel said, hoping to change the subject away from her less than ladylike intentions.

Maggie shook her head as she hung up Isobel's normal day dress. "Paintings of people I don't know. Why would I love that?"

Taking a deep breath, Isobel forced herself to remain calm. The last thing she needed to do was upset Maggie, the maid was vital to her plans. If things worked out as she hoped, having Maggie with her would provide the respectability needed. It would allow her to bend the rules without breaking them.

"Regardless," Isobel said, "We are going."

The maid continued to look at her with a doubtful glare.

"I tell you what," Isobel said as she quickly examined herself in the looking glass. "After we are done, we will go to a chocolatier, I promise you will enjoy that."

The maid's eyes grew wide with excitement. Isobel smiled internally at discovering the young woman's weakness.

"Come on," Isobel said. "While the staff is at their noon meal, we can be away before anyone notices."

Maggie snorted. "Mr. Stevenson doesn't miss much and he's going to blame me."

Isobel ignored her as she retrieved her reticule and checked that she had enough coins for the day. Locking her arm through Maggie's, she forced the woman to go with her. When they reached the top of the stairs, Isobel hesitated a moment to look over the banister and make sure no one was about.

This was the moment, she thought. If they could get outside without being seen they would be free. The thought was intoxicating. Free from judgment. Free from control. Her heart raced as the two of them snuck down the stairs.

As they reached the front door, Isobel held her breath, expecting at any moment a voice to call out, stopping them from escaping.

But there was no voice. Isobel smiled to herself as she pulled the door behind her. The final click of the lock emphasized her freedom. They had done it.

Pulling Maggie into a tight hug, Isobel bounced down the steps and towards the street corner.

As they walked, the two young women kept an eye out for anyone they might know. But Isobel was amazed at how different things were. Dressed as a common servant or tradeswoman offered a barrier to identity. It was remarkable.

Both men and woman passed them by. Everyone in a rush to be somewhere else. Cabbies did not look at them with expectant eyes, hoping for a fare. Men didn't tip their hats. In fact, some didn't even step out of the way. A surge of excitement traveled down Isobel's spine. This was a different world.

A memory of the cottage on the Brookenham estate filled her. She had been a member of the village community. Even though she was only fourteen at the time, she had felt a connection with everyone else.

That feeling had been lost when Ann married Norwich and she came to live here in London. It wasn't only a change in location though. It was a change in status. As the sister-in-law of a powerful Duke. People had treated her differently. As a separate entity, not one of them.

Five years of separation had left a hollow ache in the bottom of her stomach. That feeling of otherness. Neither a true member for the ton, yet with too much privilege to be a member of the common people.

She had missed this, she realized. This sense of being like everyone else.

"Do you really think we should take a cab, Miss?" Maggie said as Isobel tried to draw the attention of a cabbie.

Isobel nodded as another cab passed them without even acknowledging their existence.

"Maids don't normally, Miss. It is too expensive. Not unless they are on the business of their mistress, and the footman would arrange it."

Isobel frowned as she stepped out into the street.

"Miss …" Maggie gasped trying to stop her.

Shaking off the hand on her arm. Isobel stepped out enough to force a cabbie to acknowledge them and pull his horse to a halt. Being one of the average people was all fine, but she refused to walk all the way to the museum.

Isobel smiled up at the cabbie as she opened the door and indicated Maggie should get in.

The cabbie looked down at them with a deep frown, as if asking what they were thinking interfering with his business.

"The museum," Isobel said.

The cabbie continued to frown. "Two farthings," he said, obviously wanting to be paid before he would move one inch. Isobel sighed as she removed the coins from her reticule and reached up to place them in his hand. How rude, she thought. Shouldn't he have waited until after they had been delivered?

Oh well, what did it matter if it got her to the museum?

As she settled into the seat next to Maggie she glanced over and laughed. Her maid looked whiter than a summer cloud.

"I promise, this will be fun," she told her as she patted her hand.

The maid didn't even try to hide it when she rolled her eyes.

Isobel laughed and settled back, letting a sense of freedom wash over her. For three weeks, she had felt hemmed in on all sides. Between Old Stevenson, The Dowager, and worst of all, Lord Brookenham.

Somehow the man had chosen to appear at every function she attended. His large presence reminding everyone that she was under his watchful eye. Sending a heavy scowl at every man she danced with.

If she perchance talked to a man, or worse, a group of men, the Earl would appear, hovering in the background. Several times, she had seen men glance over at Lord Brookenham, then make their excuses before leaving.

It was enough to drive a woman mad.

What made it worse was that she could not confront him about it. What could she say that would change his behavior? Nothing. Norwich had obviously asked him to watch over her. If she complained to the Duke, he would solve the problem by removing her to Kent.

No, she would have to tolerate Lord Brookenham's presence. At least until she found a husband.

If she didn't know better, she would have believed The Dowager was telling the Earl where they would be. But the older woman had assured her that she hadn't.

That meant Stevenson. The traitor.

Don't be too hard on him, Isobel thought. The butler was probably only doing as he had been instructed by His Grace.

But that was why this day was so important. She needed to show some rebellion. To show everyone, especially herself, that she could not be controlled or pushed.

When the cab pulled a halt in front of the museum, Isobel stepped out and looked up at the large white building with its red roof. The seat of British culture, she thought. The home of all that was wonderful about living in this time and place.

Her heart raced as she hurried Maggie up the steps and into the huge building. Her eyes shifted left and right. Viscount Darlington had mentioned at their last dance that he planned on visiting the museum this afternoon.

Had there been a hint in his eyes. As if he hoped she would also attend.

Her heart fell a little. He wasn't there. The thought was troubling, but not devastating. What did that tell her? she wondered. Was she more excited by the idea of meeting someone without being observed by her family? Was she more interested in the idea than the man?

"This way Maggie," Isobel said as she guided her maid up the stairs. "The lower floor is the library. Books. I want to see the statues, the Greek vase collection. That is up here."

Her maid shot her a doubtful stare but joined her. As they climbed the large staircase, Isobel continued to scan the room hoping to see the Viscount. But, without luck. Would he recognize her? Not dressed as she was. No, she would have to approach him.

But it appeared that would not be necessary. The man was not there.

Had he assumed she had not realized his suggestion? Was that why he wasn't here?

It could be any of a thousand reasons she realized. In fact, he might not have been hinting at all. Perhaps it had been but a casual comment and he had changed his mind.

See, she thought. This was what happened when she over thought things. What happened when she, 'jumped to conclusions,' as Lydia called it.

Oh well, no bother. She still had an entire museum to explore.

For the next several hours she pulled Maggie from one display to another. At first, the girl seemed bored, but as Isobel explained the significance of a painting. The layers of depth expressed by the artist. Maggie slowly grew to become interested.

As they came to a particularly large Greek statue of a warrior, Isobel frowned for a moment as she thought the stone reminded her of Lord Brookenham. Her cheeks grew warm as she examined the strong male form. Wide shoulders, strong muscles. Yes, it could have been Brookenham. She could well imagine him on some distant battlefield with a javelin in his hand.

But there was more. Something about the statue's eyes as its glare followed her wherever she went in the room. Troubling. Extremely bothersome.

Unable to tolerate the cold stare, she hurried Maggie out of the room and to the next exhibit. Only when she was out of sight of the statue, was she able to relax.

Most peculiar, she thought.

Unfortunately, they were unable to finish touring before a footman walked through the gallery ringing a bell and announcing the museum would be closing soon.

"Is it time for us to visit the chocolatier's?" Maggie asked with a hopeful smile.

Isobel laughed, her heart was a little sad at the thought that she would not be able to see everything, but that only meant she would have to return. It surprised her to realize she had not thought of Viscount Darlington for hours.

In fact, she had thought of Lord Brookenham much more. That statue, for some reason, it had lodged itself in her brain and refused to leave.

As they stepped outside, she twisted first right then left as she tried to get her bearings. It had always been so much easier in the forest at home. There each tree looked different. Here in London. All of the streets appeared the same. Confusing to say the least.

"This way," she said as she started to the left, hoping it was the correct choice. If not, they would simply take a cab home. That was the beauty of London, there was always a cab available.

As the women made their way back into the heart of London, Isobel continued to twist and turn as she tried to pinpoint where she was. The thought of not stopping at the chocolatier was unthinkable. Maggie would never forgive her. Besides the thought of admitting defeat was not in her nature.

"Here," Isobel said as she started to pull Maggie down a back alley, the street she wanted was on the other end, she just knew it.

"Miss," Maggie said as she hesitated, her wide eyes looking down the alley. "This is London, remember."

Isobel laughed. It was broad daylight. There were people in the vicinity. Nothing could happen.

"Come on, we must hurry," she told her maid. "Or they will be closed and we will have to return home without stopping for chocolate."

Maggie continued to frown. But eventually, it appeared to Isobel, that her maid's love of chocolate overwhelmed her fear of the alley.

The afternoon sun sank into shadows as a cold chill passed over her shoulders. A distant sound made her jump as her heart raced. Perhaps this had not been a wise idea, she thought as they made their way deeper and deeper into the tunnel of darkness created by the alley walls.

Maggie's hand found hers, as once again, a scraping sound echoed through the narrow passage. Both of them instinctively slowed their forward progress.

Was the noise rats? The thought of rats scurrying beneath her dress sent a shudder through her entire body. She so hated rats.

Isobel glanced over her shoulder to see if it might be better to return the way they had come. But her heart jumped when a man stepped out of the shadows behind them.

He had let them pass, she thought immediately, staying hidden until they were well into the alleyway.

Her palms grew wet as her heart raced. Pulling at Maggie's hand, she started to hurry when once again another man stepped out in front of them, blocking their way. Like the other, he was dressed in rough clothes with a cloth cap pulled down low over his face.

It was his hands she couldn't avoid staring at. Big, scarred, and filthy. As if they had never been washed a day in his life. A shudder passed down her spine as the man looked up and smiled a toothless grin.

"What'a we got 'ere?" he asked with a sickening smile that sent a cold bolt of fear to her very soul. Every woman instinctively knew what that smile meant. This was an animal, a man who would take what he wanted.

"You take the dark 'aired one," the man yelled to his companion approaching from the rear. "I want the Red'ead," he added as he stared into Isobel's eyes, letting her know what he intended to do.

Maggie gasped.

Isobel swallowed hard. What had she done? A simple afternoon at a museum was going to lead to disaster.

Both men moved towards them, boxing them in. Isobel cursed herself for coming this way. Her heart pounded in her chest as she fought to stop herself from screaming. They were too far into the alley. No one would ever hear and it would only make these men even more dangerous.

Trapped, she realized as a sickening feeling filled her. Maggie didn't deserve this. No woman deserved this.

Chapter Four

Lord Brookenham cursed as he scanned up and down the street. Where had they gone? One minute they were there. He had been following from the opposite side of the street. A carriage had passed between he and the girls. And then they were gone.

Once again, he swore at the busy streets of London as he pushed his way through the traffic to get to the side of the road the two girls had been walking on.

His man Jensen had sent a runner with a message only an hour ago. It seemed Miss Isobel and her maid had snuck out of the house. Old Stevenson was going to have to do a better job.

Growling under his breath, he pushed himself through the crowd. Where had they gone? Getting Jensen's attention, he pointed back the other way. His man nodded then turned to retrace their steps.

Brookenham shook his head, he had been forced to forgo a sparring match at Big Jim's establishment and instead, spend his afternoon chasing after silly girls.

"No," he cursed to himself as he caught sight of the alleyway. Surely they wouldn't be that stupid. What could they be thinking? the idiots.

He hurried around the corner and turned into the alley. The shadows hid the distance. Had they come this way? If he followed this path, he might lose them completely.

A distant sound drew his attention. A wispy gasp that sent a cold shiver down his spine.

"Isobel?" he called out as he hurried down the alley. He had only traveled as dozen yards or so when the scene came into focus. Isobel and her maid, trapped between two brigands. Isobel had pushed her maid behind her, their backs to the wall.

He quickly assessed the situation. Neither of the women appeared to have been physically attacked. Not yet at least. No ripped clothes. No blood. As for the brigands, both looked dangerous and more than capable.

The taller of the two, on the far side, lifted a hand to try and grab Isobel by the arm. She swung at him with her reticule as she stepped out of his reach.

A fiery anger filled Brookenham as he stepped out of the shadows. "I say, gentlemen. I would advise against your plans."

Both men spun to confront this new danger. Isobel's eyes grew as big as saucers as she whispered, "Brookenham?"

Lord Brookenham ignored her, keeping his focus on the two adversaries. Both men froze, their cruel eyes narrowing, obviously despising the idea of being interrupted. He followed their eyes as they conducted a quick scan and could read their thoughts as they cataloged the situation.

A gentleman, alone, with no walking stick, and therefore no hidden sword. All in a back alley with no chance of help. The taller one smiled slowly as the facts began to register.

"I say, Jack," the taller one said. "Two pretty birds and a heavy purse. This is our lucky day."

The shorter one, obviously named Jack, only grunted as he lowered his head and charged.

Brookenham stepped back, instinctively bringing up both fists as thousands of hours practicing in the ring had taught him. This was different though. This was life and death. And if he lost, Isobel and her maid would suffer the consequences.

And there were two of them.

The attacker came in low, obviously hoping to wrap his target up so that his friend could come in and finish the job.

Brookenham refused to cooperate, stepping to the side, he threw a jab with every bit of force he could muster, aiming to punch through the man's head. His fist caught the man just in front of his ear and propelled him into the alley wall.

The taller one watched his friend slide down to his knees then fall forward. Out like a snuffed candle. The man's eyes widened in surprise as he looked at his fallen comrade then at the gentleman who had appeared out of nowhere. Obviously, this had not been a part of their plan.

Brookenham was tempted to kick the man on the ground. The rules of the ring forbade it. But this was not the ring and these men had attacked Isobel. They deserved no quarter. However, before he could address the matter. The taller one reached to his side and pulled a knife.

The flash of silver in the faint light made Brookenham's stomach clench. Isobel's sharp gasp drew the man's attention just enough to give him time to grab the man's wrist. The villain immediately took Brookenham's other wrist in an iron grip. Holding him back.

Twisting and turning the two of them grappled, both trying to overpower the other. Brookenham looked into the man's eyes and froze. This was a fight to the death. The man's eyes were those of a predator who knew if he lost, he would hang. There was to be no Marquis of Queensbury rules in this fight. One would live, one would die.

The attacker twisted his hand, bringing his blade to point down at Brookenham. Inches from his face. Slowly, the blade drew closer and closer as the man smiled with triumph. Brookenham pushed back. The man was as strong as a bull and determined to shove the blade into his enemy and end this once and for all.

A sick feeling filled Brookenham as he realized the man might actually do it. His heart raced as he fought for breath. No, this could not be allowed to happen. With every bit of his will, he stopped the slow descent of the blade towards him.

His muscles screamed with pain as he tried to lock his arm to hold off the attack. But once again, the blade started to descend until the point pierced his skin with a sharp pain.

"NO!" Isobel yelled as she rushed forward and kicked the man in the back of the knee.

The attacker's leg gave out from beneath him as he swung backwards. Knocking Isobel to the ground.

An anger exploded inside Brookenham as he twisted so that he could bring his right hand down with a heavy overhand punch that sent a solid crack sound echoing off the alley walls.

Twisting, he grabbed the knife arm and brought it down over his knee like a piece of kindling. The man yelled with pain as the knife scuttered over the cobblestones.

Brookenham didn't think, his animal instincts took over as he dropped the man then reached back and kicked him in the head. To hell with manners. The man deserved to die. Growling, he kicked the man in the stomach then dropped down and wrapped his fingers around the man's neck.

"My Lord, no," Isobel said as she grabbed his shoulder and tried to pull him away. "James, no. You can't."

Slowly, awareness returned. No, he shouldn't kill the man. The authorities would become involved. Isobel would be tainted with scandal. It was for that reason alone that he let Isobel pull him away from the unconscious man beneath him.

"My Lord, please."

He pushed away and stood up. Taking a deep breath, he fought to calm his racing heart and the anger coursing through him.

"We should go, Miss," Isobel's maid said as she looked down at the two men laying in the alley. "Before anyone sees you here. The stories ..."

Isobel ignored her maid as she slowly reached up to brush a gloved finger at the wound in his cheek from the brigand's knife. She studied it for a moment then slowly shook her head.

"Thank you," she said as she pulled a handkerchief from her reticule and wiped at his bloody cheek.

Brookenham hesitated for a moment as a thousand emotions washed through him. Anger mixed with guilt for allowing this to happen mixed with something else. A fear of what might have been.

"Your maid is correct. We need to be away."

Isobel frowned for a moment then looked down at their attackers.

"What about them?"

"You can't afford to be associated with this. We must leave them."

"But ..."

"His Lordship is right, Miss. Please, we must go," the maid said as she started to pull Isobel down the alley and away from the carnage.

"Come," Brookenham said. "I will get us a cab to take you home."

Isobel frowned as she hesitated. Obviously upset at the lack of justice, but finally she nodded as she realized it was their only choice. Taking a deep breath, the young woman followed her maid back down the alley, occasionally looking over her shoulder at him. Her brow furrowed in a strange look. As if she was trying to solve an unsolvable problem.

When they reached the end of the alley, Brookenham took a moment to ensure his clothes were adjusted correctly and that his cravat was still tied correctly. No one should ever question his appearance. Once he was sure things were as they should be, he stepped out into the street and hailed a cab large enough for the three of them.

As he climbed up into the cab, Isobel gave him a hesitant glance. Like a little girl who had been caught sneaking a dessert before dinner.

Glancing over at her maid, Brookenham shook his head, "We will talk of this when you are once again safely at home."

Isobel sighed heavily as she nodded. He could tell that she knew her errors but that was not going to stop him from pointing them out. Each and every one. And he would continue to do so until she agreed to never allow herself to be   put   in   such   danger   again.

Chapter Five

Isobel bit down on the inside of her mouth as the cab pulled to a stop in front of her home. Her heart continued to race with the realization of just how close Maggie and herself had come to true disaster.

And then, the thought of Lord Brookenham being scarred for life, all because she had wanted to visit the museum. She had been so foolish, she thought as a sense of guilt filled her.

"Here," Brookenham said to the cabbie as he handed up some coins.

Isobel used his distraction to hurry down out of the cab and up the steps to the front door, Maggie close behind. As she reached for the doorknob, the large oak door was pulled open by Old Stevenson.

The butler shot her a blustering stare as if she had betrayed England itself.

Gritting her teeth, she pushed past the butler and started up the stairs to her room.

"No, you don't," Lord Brookenham barked from behind her. "We are not done."

She turned slowly as Maggie shot her a concerned look that also let her know she was on her own for this one.

"The parlor," His lordship said as he pointed across the entryway like a vengeful God.

Isobel swallowed hard. This could not be avoided. Glancing into his eyes she shuddered, the man was furious and fighting to hold back his anger.

His expression softened as he turned to Maggie, "Will you please prepare Miss Isobel a bath?"

Maggie smiled with relief as she gave a quick curtsy before rushing up the stairs. Isobel looked after her as envy filled her. The woman was going to get off scot-free while she bore the brunt of His Lordship's wrath.

Lord Brookenham continued to stand there like a giant oak tree. Refusing to be moved as he continued to point to the parlor.

She took a deep breath, lifted the hem of her dress and slowly made her way to the parlor. With each step, she felt the dread building inside of her. Why did it have to be this man? If Norwich or Ann were to chastise her, she would have taken it in stride.

But the thought of this man pointing out her many failings this day sent a cold chill through her. A shudder passed through her when she thought of Ann and Norwich learning about the incident. She hated disappointing them. It was her worst fear.

Or at least had been until today. Now she knew what true fear felt like, she doubted she would ever look at things the same again. That cold dead feeling that had filled her as her mind raced with all the things that could be done to her and Maggie.

No, she would never look at the world the same way again.

Forcing her feet to cross the entryway, she went into the parlor and turned to face her nemesis. Let him say his words she thought. Let him get it all out. Heaven knew, he had earned the right.

When he had appeared out of nowhere to save them, Isobel had felt her world shift. As if some knew strange awareness had settled over her. Then, to watch him fight two men, defeating them both. To see him injured like that had torn at her insides, especially when she realized it was only because of her that he had been in such a situation.

No, the man had earned the right to yell at her.

Taking a deep breath, she lifted her chin and set her shoulders, she stood there, ready for the onslaught.

Brookenham stepped into the room, his eyes on hers. He reached behind him and slammed the door, making her jump.

His angry scowl continued to stare at her, as if he were trying to mine the inside of her brain for some understanding of how she could be so stupid.

The two of them continued to look at each other until Isobel could hold his stare no longer and looked down at the ground in defeat. He was right, she had been a fool.

A heavy sigh brought her attention back to the man before her. His expression had softened, however.

"Are you well?" he asked.

Isobel frowned. "I assure you, My Lord, my mind is perfectly sound."

He laughed and shook his head. "That is up for debate. No, I meant, were you injured in any way? By those men?"

Isobel balked for a moment at the tenderness in his voice.

"No," she answered as she brought a hand up to her cheek where the attacker had hit her, knocking her to the ground. "No, not really, and I believe Maggie is uninjured as well."

Lord Brookenham nodded as he placed his hands behind his back and began to pace.

Isobel held her breath as the tension began to rise. She watched the large man walk back and forth as he wrestled with something inside of him. What? she wondered. Why didn't he simply yell and scream at her? Point out her many failings. Then the two of them could go on with their lives as they always had.

"Miss Isobel," he began, his voice much softer than she expected. In fact, she almost flinched it seemed to tender.

"Please," he continued, "in the future, do strive to avoid such situations."

She froze as her brow narrowed in confusion. Where were the harsh words? Where were the recriminations about her lack of intelligence? The cuts, the put-downs. This tenderness was almost worse.

"Lord Brookenham ..." she began.

He held up a hand stopping her from continuing.

"I believe we should keep this matter between us. Can your maid be trusted?"

"Maggie?" Isobel asked with a frown. "Of course."

He nodded. "Then not a word, not to your friends, not to The Dowager ..."

She shuddered at the thought.

"... I will not send word to Norwich. There is nothing he could do to change things. So, there is no need. I am sure word will get back to him that you snuck out without an escort other than your maid. But there is no need for him to know about those men in the alley. It would upset your sister, and we don't want that at the moment."

She sighed heavily, was she really going to be able to avoid disappointing her family. What was even more important. She would be allowed to remain in London. The thought of being pulled away had bothered her more than she realized. Time was running out. She needed to find a husband and that would not happen at Norwich's country estate.

"But," he continued in a calm voice, "I must have your word that you will not do something so idiotic again. That you will realize that if you had simply taken a footman, this could have been avoided."

She cringed with guilt. But still, she felt the need to push back.

"A footman would have reported ..." she stopped talking as she realized how close she had come to admitting that the entire fiasco was a result of her wanting to meet Lord Darlington. No, that would not go over well.

Lord Brookenham frowned

"... Of course, My Lord," she said. "I give you my word, I will not sneak away unless I am fully escorted."

He sighed heavily, obviously relieved that she was not going to put up a fight about the matter.

Isobel's shoulder's slumped with relief as she realized it was over. All of it, the fear in the alley. The terror of watching this man fight for her life. The anxiety about being chastised. Wondering how The Dowager and Norwich would react. All of it was behind her.

A sense of calm washed over her as she looked at Lord Brookenham. How had he known they were there. For the first time, the thought entered her mind. Had he been following them. How? Why?

No, she would have seen him. The man stuck out in a crowd. Head and shoulders above everyone else, it would have been impossible.

She was tempted to confront him on the matter, but that would open the issue again and she had just achieved resolution. No, it was too dangerous.

Instead, she looked at him.

"You are bleeding, My Lord," she said as she stepped towards him. His hand came up to his cheek then he shrugged.

"Just a moment," she said as she reached around him and opened the door. "A wash basin and bandages," she said to Stevenson. The butler nodded then hurried off.

When but a few seconds later there was a knock at the door, she opened it and took the china bowl and bundle of clean bandages from the Lizzy, the downstairs maid and closed the door before anyone else could enter.

She wanted to do this alone. A need inside of her demanded that she be the person to nurse him.

"Sit," she said as she nodded to a chair. "You are too tall for me to do the job right."

He laughed as he sat down, looking up at her with a curious frown.

Isobel dipped a bandage in the water and then slowly turned to him. Their eyes locked for a moment as she hesitated, her hand but a hairsbreadth from his cheek.

Swallowing hard, she forced her racing heart to calm down as she gently wiped at the wound on his cheekbone, just beneath his eye. Her insides shuddered as she realized how close he had come to truly being injured.

"I should call a doctor," she said as her fingers paused, his eyes had captured hers.

"No, need," he said, his breath caressing her cheek.

She took a deep breath then returned to cleaning the wound. Then forced herself to step back.

"It might scar," she said without looking away from his eyes.

He shrugged his shoulders. "I will tell people I got it during fencing practice. Or better yet, a duel. That will impress the ladies."

Isobel snorted, "You impress the ladies more than enough as it is."

The two of them held each other's stare for a long moment. Isobel felt her heart racing and a strange need building up inside of her.

What was it about this man that made her life so complicated?

"Yes, ... Well," Brookenham began, interrupting her thoughts, pulling her out of her dream-like state. "I should be going. If I hurry, I can finish the things I had planned on doing before being interrupted."

A sense of guilt flashed through her.

"Thank you again, My Lord," she said. "And I promise, no more drama."

He frowned as he shook his head, obviously not completely believing her.

"Take care, Miss Stafford. It would upset your sisters if anything happened to you."

As she tried to decipher his words, he turned and disappeared from the room. Leaving her there to try and understand the thousand emotions running through her body.

Chapter Six

Lord Brookenham checked his cravat in a hall mirror then stepped into the ballroom. Another gala, another night. It really was becoming bothersome.

Of course, there were benefits. Several widows had let it be known they would be willing to share his bed. He smiled to himself. What more could a man ask for? Willing women with no need for commitments.

No, he reminded himself. He was here to keep an eye on Miss Isobel and she was determined to find a husband.

She and The Dowager had accepted almost every invitation. Granted, he probably didn't have to attend each one. Isobel had been on her best behavior since the incident in the alley. But it was only a matter of time. Besides, it wasn't Isobel that concerned him.

It was the gaggle of idiots that flocked around her. Each one was a disaster in waiting. Men he wouldn't have trusted to hold his horse, let alone marry a friend's ward.

What did she find so interesting about such men? Especially Darlington, he thought as he sighted the man across the room. Clenching his fists, he forced himself to remain calm. The man was a Viscount after all. But there was something about him that rubbed the wrong way.

Maybe it was the way he treated the staff at the club. Short, rude, without consideration. Or the way he rode his horse, imperious without a care for the animal. But there was more, the rumors were particularly worrisome.

Men talked, and from what he had heard, Lord Darlington had a reputation for physical confrontation with women of the night. In fact, it was said that Madam DePaul herself had banned him from her institution.

It took a particular type of evil to be banned from a brothel.

Brookenham pulled his gaze away from the man in question and scanned the room until he found Isobel and The Dowager talking with several other young women by the French doors to the garden.

His insides relaxed. Isobel looked particularly beautiful in a forest green dress. As she did at all of these events. Why wasn't the woman married? The men of the ton were not idiots. They could see her worth. No. That was not the problem. More than one man had indicated interest according to The Dowager. No, there was something about Isobel. She was unable to find her match.

If the girl didn't hurry, she would find herself on the shelf. Passed by as younger, newer girls joined the hunt. Or worse. The only candidates would be old men, young fops, or penniless trolls.

Sighing to himself, he started towards Isobel and The Dowager. Since the alley incident, he preferred to let them know he was there.

"My Lord," she said as she dipped into a curtsey.

"Your Grace, Miss Isobel," he replied as he bowed.

"Really Brookenham," The Dowager said as she shook her head. "I never knew you enjoyed dancing so much. We seem to find you at every event. If I didn't know better, I would assume you were searching for a wife."

Several of the other young ladies in the group smiled and batted their eyelashes at him. Isobel's eyes grew wide at the brazenness of The Dowager.

He held back a shudder. Why did things always seem to come back to his lack of a wife?

"That is not my intention, I can assure you," he said with enough conviction that there should be no doubt in anyone's mind.

The Dowager laughed, "It would make your dear mother so happy. She was telling me just the other day that she fears she will never have grandchildren."

Brookenham bit his tongue, he was not going to get into a discussion with The Dowager about this matter. It was bad enough dealing with his mother.

An awkward silence fell over the group. Several of the women were looking at him from behind their fans. He was well used to this. The target of empty-headed women with but one thing on their mind. A husband.

Each of them looked at him as a prize to be won. A solution to all of their problems. In some cases, he would be expected to support their family as well.

Only Isobel looked at him differently. She saw him as he was. A confirmed bachelor, friend of the family. And best of all, not on her list of potential husbands.

"Might I have a dance?" he asked her out of the blue. "If you have any available of course."

Her eyebrows shot up. Obviously surprised, he never asked her to dance. Not since she had been a young girl of fourteen and had criticized his ability.

"I do, My Lord," she answered. "The first one, a quadrille is open."

"Excellent," he said as the musicians began to ready their instruments. "Shall we?" he said as he held out his arm.

Isobel's brow furrowed in confusion as she took his arm and let him lead her to the dance floor.

"I do hope I have improved since the last time we danced," he said.

She gasped, her face going white. "You remember that? I do apologize, I was a silly girl."

He laughed. But decided not to press the point. Instead, as they arranged themselves in line and waited for the music to start, he leaned forward and whispered. "You look particularly fetching tonight. Both Darlington, and Beaverton can't keep their eyes off of you."

Her cheeks grew pink as she glanced from beneath her brow to where the two Lords in question were standing with their partners but looking at her.

Before he could say more, the music started and they came together. He smiled down at her and winked.

Isobel blushed, faltering on a step before she could pull herself together. He decided to stop teasing her and finished the dance without incident.

"Thank you, My Lord," she said. "You dance divinely."

"For an Earl, you mean."

She laughed, then instantly brought her fan up to hide it. He smiled inside, he liked making her laugh.

Things had changed between them since the incident in the alley. The quickness to anger. The disapproval judgment. It had slipped away. Perhaps not forever. But at least for now.

It was as if they had unofficially agreed to stop despising each other.

"You know," he said as he leaned down to whisper to her. "You can do better than either Darlington or Beaverton. Much better."

Isobel gasped as she pulled up short and shot him an angry gaze.

"Really My Lord, it is rather unseemly to disparage such fine gentleman."

An anger flared up inside of him. How dare she dismiss him so casually. He had been trying to help. She had automatically assumed he had some ulterior motive.

Snorting, he shook his head, "My thieving agent was more of a gentleman than those two. And he was sentenced to transport to Australia."

Isobel scowled at him, obviously upset. "Are you equating Lord Darlington and Lord Beaverton to thieves?"

He sighed internally, So much for their agreed peace. It seemed he'd breached it without intention.

"No," he said, "but there are many things that can make a man less than a gentleman. In addition to which Lord Beaverton has the backbone of a jellyfish. Not exactly husband material if you ask me."

Isobel turned on him, her hands on her hips. He could see a thousand thoughts racing through her head as she fought to maintain control inside the crowded room. The last thing she needed to do was get into an argument with Lord Brookenham in front of all these people.

He smiled to himself. He was tempted to push her a little further. Just enough so that she yelled at him. It would be interesting to hear what she had to say if she let her true feelings out.

"Isobel," The Dowager hissed as she stepped up to them.

Both Lord Brookenham and Isobel continued to stare at each other for a long moment then Isobel allowed herself to be guided away.

"The man is infuriating," she said to The Dowager as they left.

Brookenham could only stare after her, a smile on his lips. Then a sudden thought flashed into his mind. He needed to be careful. Isobel was the type of person who would do something just to prove him wrong.

In fact, she might very well marry either of the gentlemen in question just because he believed she shouldn't.

The thought sent a cold chill down his spine. Norwich would never forgive him if he allowed a man such as Darlington to marry Isobel.

.oOo.

Isobel spent the next hour trying to calm the angry monster inside of her. How dare he say that about Lord Darlington. The Viscount had been nothing but charming. By what right did Lord Brookenham disparage a man who might very well become her husband.

It was unjust. And unkind.

As for Lord Beaverton, she knew perfectly well that the man was not husband material. Especially not for her. But that didn't mean she couldn't be friendly with the man. Heaven knew few were.

No, it was Darlington that bothered her. Or Lord Brookenham's opinion of him that truly got under her skin.

Lord Darlington had been hinting of late. Dancing with her twice at each ball. Between dances, he would quite often join them. Talking about inconsequential things. Entertaining her. His manner growing more familiar.

A casual touch, a knowing glance. The man was trying to win her over with charm.

What did Lord Brookenham know anyway? The man was a male after all. Clueless. With absolutely no idea what a woman looked for in a husband. At least not what she was looking for.

Taking a deep breath, she forced herself to not grind her teeth. It was unbecoming. But the man was intolerable. Telling her who she should marry. Who was acceptable. No. It was intolerable and she must tell him again to mind his own business.

Twisting, she looked out over the crowd until she found him in the distant corner. He was so tall it was impossible to miss him. He stood out like a wolf amongst dogs. Next to him, looking up with adoring eyes was Lady Crawford, only recently out of mourning.

Such a shame, Isobel thought. So young to be a widow.

"You know, she has no chance," Lady Burton said in a slight whisper as she stepped up next to her.

Isobel frowned, surprised to see a woman she barely knew say something so... so personal about Lord Brookenham. And a widow herself.

"Why do you say that?" she asked, unable to rein in her curiosity. This was the ton after all. As The Dowager said, it was fueled by gossip.

The young Lady Burton gave a small smile. "Lord Brookenham prefers fair haired women with blue eyes."

Isobel simply raised an eyebrow as she examined the woman. Her blond hair and blue eyes made her wonder if it was simply wishful thinking on her part.

Seeing the doubt in her eyes, Lady Burton smiled with a look that made Isobel's insides turn to stone. "Didn't you know? His last two mistresses were both blond and blue eyed. I assume he will desire the same in his wife."

Isobel could only shake her head. "I would think a higher hurdle is the fact that Lord Brookenham will never marry."

The look of shock in the woman's eyes was priceless. It took every bit of effort for Isobel not to smile as if she had won a small victory.

"No," Isobel continued to drive home the win. "I have heard him tell my brother-in-law more than once that he intends for his cousin to inherit the title.

The look of shocked disbelief on Lady Burton's face was one of those moments that Isobel would remember for a long time. She was perfectly aware that Lord Brookenham had left a long line of women behind him but she refused to share gossip about the Earl with this woman.

Turning him over to this she-wolf felt as if it would be a betrayal of a family friend.

"Excuse me," Isobel said as she turned to start towards him when she saw a footman approach him with a letter on a silver platter. Lord Brookenham frowned as he thanked the footman and examined the letter before opening it.

She stopped in her approach as she watched him read the letter, his frown grew deeper with each word.

Before she could look away, he glanced up and caught her watching him. His shoulder slumped as a sad expression passed behind his eyes. Isobel's breath hitched. It was not good.

Holding her breath, she watched as he walked towards her, his eyes holding hers.

"What?" she asked as she felt the warmth drain from her face. Was it Ann, or Lydia and the new baby?

"Your Aunt Ester," he said as his eyes softened. "She has taken ill. My staff has moved her to the main house."

Isobel's heart fell. Her only relative other than her sisters. The woman who had taken them in when they were destitute. The sweet, kind, unusual woman who had been the one thing in this world that had cared whether the Stafford sisters had lived or died.

Her aunt had refused to move to London. Instead, insisting that she be allowed to remain in the small cottage on Lord Brookenham's estate.

Both Norwich and Brookenham ensured she was well taken care of. But the woman was without family.

"I must go to her," Isobel said as she began searching the room for The Dowager.

There was The Dowager standing next to Lord Darlington of all people. Hurrying across the room, she left Lord Brookenham behind her as she quickly told The Dowager the news. Lord Darlington listened closely.

The older woman frowned. "What of your season? This might be your last chance."

Isobel scoffed and waved her hand dismissively. This was Aunt Ester. Besides, if she wanted to marry, she could pick any of a dozen men. It would not be the match she wished, but she would have a family. Granted, with each passing year, the pool of candidates decreased significantly.

No, she must go to Aunt Ester.

"I will send word to my sisters. Neither Ann with the coming baby, nor Lydia with the newborn should be tasked with this. No, it is my responsibility."

"Perhaps, you would allow me to escort you, Miss Stafford," Lord Darlington said. "The King's roads are no place for a young woman such as yourself."

Isobel almost laughed. The man had no idea who she was. Not in truth. To him, she was the sister-in-law of a Duke. Not the common girl running through the forest.

"There will be no need, Darlington," Lord Brookenham said as he stepped up next to them, giving the Viscount a fierce glance. Once the message had been received, Lord Brookenham's brow softened as he turned to look down at her.

"I have need to return to my estate and will escort Miss Stafford."

Isobel saw the disappointment in Lord Darlington's eyes and the angry look he shot Lord Brookenham. Then her heart jumped as she realized that she would be forced to share a carriage with the man for hours on end. But, what choice did she have?

The question was, would they be able to make it to Brookenham without killing each other?

Chapter **Seven**

Isobel bit back a heavy sigh. It was going to be a long ride. She must keep her feelings in check she reminded herself. But there was something about the man across from her that continued to prick at her. Even just the sound of his breathing sent an uncomfortable irritation between her shoulder blades.

Simple things. Like the way he sat there as if he were one of the monoliths from Stonehenge. Calm, solid, unmovable. Or the way his eyes missed nothing. Always observant, catching every nuance.

But it was that smirk that scraped against every one of her nerves. That knowing attitude of someone who was too intelligent for his own good.

No, she must remain calm she thought for the thousandth time since they had left London. It was going to be a long day.

Glancing over at Maggie, she gave her maid a small sad smile. Isobel's heart went out to the girl. Maggie was looking a little pale as her eyes remained focused on her hands in her lap. The maid hated long carriage rides. The motion bothered her stomach.

But there was no choice in the matter. Isobel could not be left alone with Lord Brookenham. Society would never understand. And he could not allow them to travel unescorted. Therefore. the need for a maid. A witness.

The Dowager had been rather upset at the idea of Isobel traveling to Brookenham's estate. Only the fact that his mother was already there had allowed the woman to give her permission.

That and the fact that there was nothing that could have kept Isobel from attending to her ill aunt. The Dowager had wisely acquiesced to the inevitable.

Sighing, Isobel removed her shawl and folded it into a pillow then reached around Maggie to let her lean her head against the coach wall. She then pushed the curtain aside just a smidge to let in some fresh air for the girl.

Reaching over, she patted Maggie's hand and said, "Rest, it will make you feel better."

The maid sighed heavily but leaned her head against the folded cloth and closed her eyes.

Lord Brookenham raised an eyebrow and shot the maid a concerned look. Isobel could only grimace and hope things did not grow worse.

As she sat there, rocking with the sway of the coach, Isobel wondered once again why he had insisted on escorting them? Surely the needs of his estate could have been met at another time.

Leaning back in her seat, she rested her head against the squabs and looked at the man from beneath her brow. As she sat there, she felt the awkward silence grow to an almost intolerable level. That heavy, cloying silence that ate at a person's soul.

"I thank you again, Lord Brookenham, for escorting us. It really wasn't necessary," she said as a way to pierce the annoying silence.

He shrugged his massive shoulders and smirked at her. "Your Brother-in-law, Norwich, would be disappointed if I didn't."

Her brow furrowed, "I have always been curious about your friendship with the Duke. It seems more than simple manners."

He laughed gently and shrugged his shoulders again.

"You know the story of my being unexpectedly raised to the title," he said. "It was never supposed to happen. There were too many people between me and the Earldom. I was neither trained nor prepared. The Duke's assistance when it happened was invaluable."

Isobel nodded. Yes, she knew that story. It had led to her sister Ann and the Duke falling in love and the three sisters being rescued from poverty. Yes, of course she knew every detail.

"So, I am but a debt that must be repaid," she asked with a deep frown.

He laughed again and shook his head. "No, Miss Stafford. I assure you, that is not it."

She took a deep breath as she tried to understand what motivated this man.

He sighed heavily when he saw her obvious confusion. "When my brother Johnathon was killed in Portugal. Long before anyone believed I would ever become an Earl. When I was but a lost young man. A boy really. The Duke took the time, made the effort when he didn't have to."

Isobel saw something pass behind the man's eyes and realized there was more depth to him than she had perceived.

"That just tells me that you are even more in debt to His Grace. Even more, reason for you to be kind to his ward."

Lord Brookenham shook his head as he frowned. "Do you really believe I am only a gentleman because of my debt to Norwich. Do you really think so little of me?"

Isobel blanched. She had not meant it to sound so judgmental. Once again, she had put her foot in her mouth. Why did she always do that, especially with this man? He always assumed the worst of her words.

"No, My Lord," she began. "I assume you can be a gentleman whenever you chose to do so."

He gasped with mock offense. "So, you are saying that I am not innately a gentleman. That I must work at it. As if I must take on a disguise to mislead the world. That unlike the rest of the aristocracy, I am not naturally a man of taste and manners."

Isobel sighed. This was going so wrong. She had hoped to only learn a little more of the man and his motivations, but it seemed at every word, he took offense.

"No, sir, that was not what I meant," she said as she felt her cheeks grow warm with embarrassment. The man twisted her words to make her look young and foolish.

He stared at her for a long moment then winked at her as he gave her a teasing smile.

"Sir," she gasped, "it is not nice to tease people."

"I don't tease people, Miss Stafford. Just you."

Her heart jumped as she tried to understand. What was it about her that drove him to treat her that way?

As if reading her mind, he leaned forward and said, "You have always been too beautiful, and too intelligent. Graced with a rebellious spirit and an assuredness uncommon in most young women of your status. Of course, I tease you. If not me, then who?"

Her heart began to race as she stared across the cramped carriage space at the man. In all the time she had known him, he had never said such words to her. Did he really think she was intelligent?

The thought tumbled around in her head as she once again realized that for some unknown reason this man's opinion about her was important. It always had been.

He had been a Lord. Even worse, A handsome, powerful Lord and she had been but a common girl living with her sisters on his family's kindness in a leaky cottage buried in the forest.

She would never forget the first time she had seen him. She had been but a girl of fourteen, sneaking around the barn of the main estate, playing with the barn cat's new kittens when the new Earl walked into the stables as if he were a God.

She had known immediately that he was the new Lord of the manor recently arrived from London. His commanding bearing, his fine aristocratic looks. Everything informed the world of his high status.

The sunshine behind him, like a golden halo. He had marched into the barn, in control of his world. So tall, so strong.

He had not known she was there, hidden in the shadows. She had frozen. Afraid to move less he learn of her presence and ban her from the main estate. Or worse, throw her family from the cottage and into destitution.

The large man had reached down and patted Sam, the collie that ruled the stable yard. Then curried his own horse before saddling the stallion himself. He was a British Lord yet took the time to be kind to animals. Even when others weren't watching.

The next time she had seen him was at the summer dance. That fairy tale evening. The Duke of Norwich had arranged their invitation because of Ann. Yet both she and Lydia had been allowed to attend.

A girl of but fourteen being allowed into the adult world for the first time.

She could still remember the shock and awe when they had entered the main house. The beauty and nobility of every room.

But, nothing had prepared her for what happened next. Unexpectedly, The Earl of Brookenham himself had asked her, an unknown girl, to dance. Isobel had been dumbfounded. She had only realized later that he had asked her so that he could avoid offending the other women in attendance.

By choosing her he had shown no favoritism. The Earl's first dance would be forgotten and become of no significance. There would be no evil stares or loud whispers. No jealousy. No, he'd chosen a little girl. What could be more inoffensive than that?

Even more important. It was his way of telling the world that he was not looking for a wife. That the woman of the district needed to adjust their thinking.

But she remembered that dance. She would always treasure it. The feeling of being treated as a grown woman. For the first time, she had felt special in her own right. Not because she was the baby of the family. Not because she was one of the Stafford sisters.

No, because an Earl had danced with her. What girl wouldn't remember that?

Biting back a sigh, she glanced across at him as he pulled the curtain back to look out at the passing scenery. The morning light shining off his fine cheekbones.

Why had they become such antagonists? She wondered. What was it about him that drove her mad with frustration.

Her thoughts were interrupted by a soft moan from Maggie.

Isobel's heart ached at her maid's distress.

Glancing over at the empty space next to Lord Brookenham a plan began to form in her mind. Looking up at him she raised an eyebrow in question.

He read her thoughts immediately and shrugged his shoulders. It was her decision, he was telling her.

Isobel nodded to herself as she stood in the swaying carriage and lifted Maggie's feet up onto the bench. Perhaps if the girl could become comfortable she might rest.

"Relax," Isobel said to her maid as she maneuvered in the tight space. Of course, the coachman chose that particular moment to find the biggest pothole available.

The carriage lurched and Isobel found herself thrown onto Lord Brookenham's lap. She gasped as his strong arms instinctively wrapped around her, holding her safe against his chest.

"Careful, Miss Stafford,"

Her breath left her as she was filled with embarrassment. But a feeling of safety and security quickly pushed aside the shame. A person could grow to love this, she realized as she felt herself threaten to sink into the strong male form surrounding her.

NO! she thought as she scrambled off of his lap and onto the seat next to him.

"I am sorry, My Lord," she said as she stared down at the floor

He laughed. "Believe me, Isobel, there are worse things in life than having a pretty girl fall into your lap. I will survive."

Her cheeks grew hot and she knew she was blushing. A fact that made her even more upset and blush even more intensely.

What was it about this man that made her so angry? Would she ever know that answer? Probably not, she realized. But now she had another concern. The memory of what it had felt like to have Lord Brookenham hold her in his arms. It was a memory that she feared would never leave her.

.oOo.

Lord Brookenham looked down at the girl resting her head on his shoulder and shook his head. The girl was beautiful in every way. Her heart-shaped face looked angelic. Especially as she slept.

The memory of holding her on his lap filled his mind and refused to leave. The soft curves had fit perfectly. As if an artist had sculpted the perfect female to fit against him in all the right places.

Swallowing hard, he tried to push away the thoughts dancing in his head. Norwich would kill him if he could see inside his mind at the moment. Even worse, Isobel would tear a strip off his hide if she ever learned about the pictures he had conjured.

No. This was Norwich's ward and besides, it was Isobel. A man shouldn't have such thoughts about such an innocent.

The coach rocked making Isobel shift. He lifted his arm to wrap around her shoulders and bring her in closer, hopefully making her comfortable. Half the old biddies of the ton would be apoplectic if they could see them now. An Earl with his arm around a young woman. They would have him married off within the week.

Thankfully, they were in a dark carriage on a back road far from London.

Glancing over at the maid across from them he smiled and shook his head. It was wrong to wish ill upon the girl. But the maid's distress had definitely livened his afternoon.

Yes, a man could get used to this.

As they continued on, he found himself smiling for no reason. Really, James, he thought. It was a good thing that the woman despised him or a simple carriage ride might lead to something they would both regret. No, he was against matrimony and that was the only way any man would ever be allowed to possess Isobel.

Sighing at the ridiculousness of his thoughts, he rested his head against the squabs and closed his eyes.

No, the sooner she was married off the better for everyone concerned. Of course, once that happened, he could stop having to keep a watchful eye over her and could return to living the life of a bachelor enjoying the finer points of London's nightlife.

Yes, that was the answer, get her married off. Preferably to a good man. Some kind, poor Baron perhaps. Or even a solid merchant. Someone who could deal with her biting tongue. Anyone but Darlington.

He smiled to himself again. That was the beauty of having her out in the country. The damn Viscount was no longer a part of her world. Sometimes, things did work out as they were supposed to.

Chapter Eight

Isobel woke with a start as the carriage pulled to a halt.

"We are here," the Earl said softly as he looked down at her with a comforting smile.

Isobel frowned as she tried to place herself then her heart lurched as she realized with shock that she was cradled in his arm.

Gasping, she pushed away, sitting up straight as she wiped at her mouth to make sure she had not drooled all over his fine coat.

"I am sorry, My Lord," she whispered as she felt her cheeks once again erupt with warmth. What was it about this man that made her blush more than a school girl with a rake?

He laughed as he nodded then reached and adjusted her bonnet. She froze as his fingers brushed her cheek. Such a tender moment. Then the door was pulled open by the footman and the true world crashed down upon them.

"Brookenham, Miss Stafford," a high pitched voice called to them from the front steps to the main house. Isobel sighed, The Earl's mother, Lady Brookenham. Isobel's stomach fluttered with worry. The woman had never been particularly kind. Not harsh, not rude, but never friendly.

Brookenham gave her a wan smile then turned to address his mother.

Isobel screwed up her courage and stepped down from the coach, immediately dropping into a curtsey for Lady Brookenham. The Countess barely acknowledged her, her face in a frown. As if an unwanted smell had invaded her house.

Isobel pushed aside any sense of hurt or injury. There was no time for such things. Instead, she turned to Mr. Wesley, the butler, she asked, "How is my Aunt Ester?"

The butler blanched, quickly glancing at Lady Brookenham for guidance.

"The doctor has assured us that we are doing everything possible to make her comfortable," the countess said.

Isobel's heart fell as her stomach clenched into a tight ball. Aunt Ester could not be ill. No, it wasn't right, the woman was too important.

The butler smiled sadly, "We have placed her in the green bedroom and you will be adjoining her in the blue. If that is acceptable?"

"I thank you, so much, My Lady," Isobel said to the countess. "You have been so kind. Both of you," she added to the Earl.

Lord Brookenham bowed slightly then indicated they should enter the house.

Isobel lifted the hem of her dress and followed the butler into the house and up the stairs to her aunt's room. Reaching the bedroom door, she took a deep breath and stepped in. She had been dreading this moment since they had left London.

Her heart squeezed tight. Her Aunt Ester looked so frail, asleep in the big fluffy bed. A maid at her bedside keeping watch.

Taking a deep breath, Isobel forced herself to move closer. The woman looked wan, her skin had a yellowish tinge and her breaths were short and fast. Her gray hair was spread across the pillow like a silver fan.

"Did the doctor say what it was?" Isobel asked without taking her eyes off the older woman.

"He was unsure," the Countess said from behind her. "He believed that your aunt was having difficulty with her heart. But the cause was unknown. Janice her cook and housekeeper assures me that your aunt was well until a few days ago."

"Once we received word," the butler said. "We had her moved here at once."

Isobel sighed heavily as she took her aunt's hand and sat down in the now vacated chair next to the bed.

Her Aunt Ester, she thought as she slowly shook her head. This was so not right. The woman was sweet, kind, and a savior. It wasn't right that she should suffer any of life's travails. Why hadn't they forced her to move to London? Or perhaps one of the sisters should have remained here with her.

Regardless, she should never have been left alone. The sense of guilt that washed through Isobel was almost overwhelming. While she had been dancing and enjoying herself in London, her aunt had grown ill.

Isobel wiped a tear. The woman had literally saved their lives. Taking them in when they had no one else in all of Britain. If not for her, they would have been cast onto the streets of Birmingham. And every girl knew what that meant. There was only one way to survive in such a world.

Swallowing hard, Isobel leaned forward and kissed her aunt's cheek. "Please," she whispered. "Please get well."

When her aunt did not respond, Isobel sat back in her chair and waited.

A little while later Maggie came in, looking refreshed now that she was no longer being rocked back and forth in the carriage.

"Your room is ready, Miss," the maid said. "And I have asked them to prepare a bath. In your room. It should be ready shortly."

"I can't leave my aunt."

Maggie smiled softly. "I will sit with her. You need to take a bath and rest Miss. Dinner will be served shortly. I believe the Countess will expect you to attend."

Isobel was tempted to balk. The guilt and shame burning inside of her told her to remain with her aunt, but Maggie was right, as usual.

The Countess would expect her at dinner. The thought made Isobel smile for the first time since arriving.

Five years earlier, there was every chance that she would have ended up as a scullery maid in Her Ladyship's kitchens. Now, because of her sister's marriage to a Duke. She was expected to sit with the Countess and her son, Lord Brookenham, in the fine dining hall. Served by butlers and footmen. Oh, how things had changed.

While she still thought of herself as the same person, everyone else looked at her differently. All because of her association with a Duke.

Thanking Maggie, she gave her aunt one last look before going into her room for her bath. Was this her aunt's deathbed? Should she tell Ann and Lydia so they could come say their goodbye's?

No, she thought. They would wait. She would wait until the morning and see if there was any improvement.

Sighing to herself, she left her aunt and pushed down the guilt and sorrow that fought to take over her emotions. No, she would be strong. Her aunt Ester would expect nothing less.

.oOo.

Lord Brookenham poured himself his second whiskey then turned to stare into the fireplace while he waited to be summoned to dinner.

The door opened behind him but he continued to stare into the flames.

"Really, Brookenham," his mother said as she stepped into the room and closed the door behind her. "Escorting that girl, yourself. You have a dozen servants that could have done the job perfectly well."

He frowned. "She is the ward of my very good friend. This is my home. Of course, I escorted her."

His mother slowly shook her head. "You need to be married. This house needs a Countess. You need an heir. Being seen with a young woman like that. A commoner ..."

"Mother," he interrupted. "Be careful. I will not have you being disparaging of Miss Stafford."

His mother waved her hand. "Oh, it is not Isobel that bothers me. She is a perfectly fine young woman. Especially for someone of her status. But she is not a Lady and you, an Earl, you need more."

His brow knit in confusion. "Mother, Miss Isobel Stafford is not a potential candidate. I assure you. Do you know how I know? Because there are no candidates. I will not be marrying."

The countess gasped, "Brookenham. Of course, you must marry. And when you do. It will be to a Lady from a noble family."

He smiled wanly. It bothered him to distress her but it was time for her to accept the truth.

"No, mother. Cousin Abernasth will make a perfect Earl if it comes to that. And he has three sons. There is no fear of the title reverting back to the crown I assure you."

His mother continued to stare at him as if he had just betrayed Great Britain itself. He could see her biting the inside of her cheek to stop herself from saying what she truly wished to tell him. He held her stare, daring her to say the words. It was important that she understand.

"It has been a long day," she said. "We will discuss this later."

He laughed and shook his head. There was no talking to the woman. He would never convince her. Instead, he would simply avoid the matter altogether. Eventually, she would come to accept the fact.

A knock at the door was followed by Wesley stepping in and informing them that dinner was served.

"Please inform Miss Stafford," he told the butler.

"I am here, My Lord," Isobel said as she stepped in behind Wesley.

His heart jumped. The woman was as beautiful as ever. Even with sad eyes and a deep frown.

"Your aunt?" he asked her.

Isobel frowned even deeper and shook her head. "I do not know, My Lord. There has been no change."

He frowned as he accepted her report. Then, turning to his mother, he held out his arm to escort her into dinner.

As they were seated, he looked again at Isobel and sighed. Dressed in a green gown, her auburn hair up, a simple gold necklace around her neck. She looked as beautiful as any Lady in all of England.

It tore at him though. To see the sadness in her eyes. Isobel was never sad, never morose. No, she was filled with energy. With a willing attitude that looked at the world as if it was hers. To see this side of her pulled at him.

"I had scheduled a party, in a few weeks," the Countess said as she swallowed a spoonful of soup. "The invitations have already been sent. Friends from London."

"Mother," Brookenham said. "Perhaps this is not the time."

"No, My Lord," Isobel interjected. "No, please do not make any changes because of myself or my aunt. I could never accept that. If necessary, we could move back to the cottage."

The Countess studied her for a moment then said, "Perhaps she will be well by then and it will not be an issue. We can but pray."

Isobel continued to stare down at her meal.

"There will be no need to move back to the cottage," the Earl said as he gave his mother a stern look. "This place is more than big enough. How many people have you invited?"

His mother shrugged her shoulders. "Lord and Lady Everton, Baron Wheaton and his wife, Lady Sheffieil and her daughter Lady Burton. Of course, at something like this, there are always others who show up. Probably no more than ten or so."

Brookenham nodded to Isobel, "We have more than enough room. There will be no need to disturb your aunt. And I am positive that your aunt will be well on the way to recovery by then."

Isobel gave him a sad smile as she nodded slightly accepting his kindness.

"Do you really intend to stay for that long?" his mother asked him. "It is not like you to miss so much of the season. Aren't you needed in Parliament?"

He shook his head. No, Norwich had asked him to watch over Isobel and he would continue to do so. Besides, a few weeks in the country might be just what he needed.

Isobel gave him a strange look then blushed when he caught her staring at him. Quickly looking down at her food, her cheeks grew a pretty shade of pink.

He forced himself to not smile. There was something about a beautiful woman's blush that could make the entire world seem a better place.

.oOo.

After dinner, Isobel excused herself so that she could return to her aunt. Both His Lordship and the Countess assured her that they understood.

As she walked up the stairs her mind whirled with a thousand different emotions. The worry about Aunt Ester, the confusion about why was Lord Brookenham being nice to her. He had neither criticized nor teased her all day. It was disconcerting, to say the least.

She wondered if there was some ulterior motive. Did he believe Aunt Ester would not recover and that was why? Or was it simply that he had grown bored with her already?

Oh, how she wished Ann or Lydia were here so that she could discuss the matter with them and so that they could help her with Aunt Ester. It felt so wrong for her to be the one making the decisions. That was Ann's job. She had always been the oldest sister. Always the one in charge.

Isobel sighed as she entered her aunt's room.

"Thank you," she told Maggie.

The maid smiled at her and nodded to her mistress's room. "Let me help you out of that dress Miss and then you can return. Your aunt will be perfectly fine for a few minutes."

Isobel took a deep breath then nodded.

Once she was changed into a more comfortable day dress, she took up her position next to her aunt's bed. What should she do? What could she do?

Please, she prayed. Please help her get well.

Chapter Nine

The next morning, Aunt Ester roused enough to recognize her. Isobel's heart swelled with happiness. Her aunt was not out of the woods yet. But there was hope.

She slowly fed her aunt broth as she told her all about London, Lydia's new baby, and a hundred other stories to keep the woman entertained. But eventually, her aunt fell back to sleep and Isobel was able to relax.

"See," Maggie said as she took the bowl of broth from her. "I knew she would get better."

"We will see," Isobel said as she studied her aunt, "We will see."

As the days progressed, her aunt slowly did improve. Sitting up in bed, even smiling occasionally. Slowly, Isobel was able to relax and even sneak away while her aunt rested in the afternoon.

After a week of nursing, Isobel felt the walls of the green bedroom begin to close in. She informed Maggie that she was going for a walk.

Maggie's eyes rose in surprise.

"This is Brookenham, not London," she told the maid. "I assure you I will be fine. Don't forget, I know these woods."

The maid held her tongue but continued to look doubtful. Isobel ignored her. She needed air, she needed an opportunity to breath.

As she made her way through the apple orchard, she couldn't help but smile. Aunt Ester was on the mend. The sky was blue and a cool breeze blew through the trees. Home, deep down, this place would always feel like home.

She wondered if after she married, would she ever have this same feeling for her husband's home.? Some other man's estate? Would it call up that sense of belonging? That sense of safety and contentment?

No, it was doubtful. But those feelings would be replaced by the love for her children. Watching them grow up. Creating a sense of home for them. That would be more than enough.

It was time she chose a husband, she realized. She could no longer hope some Prince Charming would come in and sweep her up onto his steed. She was growing old. It was time that she realized she would never find a true love. No, she must come to accept that her best option, her only option, was to settle for good enough.

A sadness filled her as she left the orchard on the trail to the cottage.

It was her only option. Choosing from the men available. She could no longer rely upon

Norwich's generosity. And if she ever hoped to have a family, she needed to accept reality.

But who? Darlington? Beaverton? Or perhaps Lord Stonewhich? He came with a ready made family, three young motherless children.

As she walked, she pondered each candidate and a dozen more. But none excited her. None really called to her.

Perhaps it would be Darlington after all. The man was exceedingly handsome. Their children would be beautiful. He was intelligent. Able to converse without fumbling for words. Yet something in the back of her head told her to hesitate. To hold off.

"No," she said to herself as she opened the gate to the cottage fence. She needed to make a decision. "When I get back to London," she mumbled to herself.

"When you get back to London. What?" Lord Brookenham asked from the cottage door.

Isobel gasped and stepped back. She had been so lost in her own thoughts she hadn't even seen him there.

"I do apologize," His Lordship said. "I came to examine the repairs to the roof. It seems that every winter creates new leaks."

Isobel continued to stare at him, unable to look away. Roof, he was talking about the roof.

"Of course, My Lord."

He stepped aside, holding the door open for her. "I assume you wish to inspect the house as well," he said. "I will leave you alone."

"No, My Lord," she blurted out, perhaps a little too quickly. The thought of him leaving because of her was distressing. She and her family already owed him so much. It would be churlish to be unthankful or worse, a burden.

Squeezing past him and into the house, she felt her body hum with energy.

"Um ... I am only here to retrieve some books for my aunt," she managed to say once she was past him.

His brow furrowed for a moment. "Miss Isobel, you must be aware that our library is open to yourself and your aunt. You are our guests."

Isobel smiled, "Of course, My Lord. But these are Aunt Ester's favorites. She will rest easier having me read them to her."

The tall Lord looked down at her with concern and a tenderness that surprised her. For the first time, she realized they were alone. Completely alone. No mothers or Dowagers. No maids. Just the two of them alone in a country cottage deep in the woods.

Their eyes locked. She realized that he had become aware of the situation as well. A nervousness began to build inside of her. A fluttery need began to burn deep in her soul.

Was he going to kiss her? Now? Here? The thought had no sooner arrived than she realized how much she wanted it to happen. Her first kiss.

Her body swayed forward, he leaned down.

Both of them drawn together. Their lips but a hair's breadth from each other. She instinctively closed her eyes as she took in the manly scent of sandalwood and leather. Yes, she thought, finally.

But, she felt him draw away. Her eye sprang open in surprise. How? Why?

"Excuse me, Miss Isobel," he said, unable to look directly into her eyes. "I must be going."

Her heart fell. He had rejected her. He had found her wanting and not worth kissing. The misery could not be kept from her eyes. She knew that he saw the pain which only made things worse. An anger flashed inside of her. How dare he reject her?

Lord Brookenham grimaced then turned and left. She watched him pass through the gate and down the path. His back ramrod straight. His wide shoulders firmly set. But he did not look back. Did not even so much as glance over his shoulder. No, she was not significant enough for that.

Her heart continued to pound in her chest as she fought to bring herself under control. She had seen it in his eyes. He had wanted to kiss her. She couldn't be mistaken. It was impossible. Yet he had pulled back.

Why? Was it her? Or, perhaps her status? No, Noblemen used common girls all the time. That couldn't be it. What then? Did he find her too plain? He had said otherwise, but perhaps that had been but a lie. A common kindness.

Or something else. Did he fear that she was trying to trap him into marriage? No, surely not. Surely, he didn't see her as that type of woman.

What then? A doubt and sorrow filled her. No wonder she was having difficulty finding her true love. Men found her repulsive. It was only men of desperation and poverty that were interested in her.

A sadness filled her as she turned to go back into the house and retrieve the books. She was a fool. She should find a husband at once. Before they were all gone. Her silly dreams of finding the perfect match must be put aside.

No, she was but a common, country miss. With nothing to offer, she reminded herself. She should take the first honest offer she received and be thankful for it.

.oOo.

Lord Brookenham shook his head as he stepped into the orchard on his way back to the manor. What had he been thinking?

The girl was an innocent with no awareness of the impact she had on men. To use her would be wrong on so many levels.

A betrayal of his best friend. A breach of every rule and custom of his people. A failure of character and an abuse of Isobel.

No, he thought. He could not allow such as thing.

Taking a deep breath, he halted for a moment and forced himself to regain control. The girl had surprised him. That was it. He had not been prepared.

But seeing her step through the gate of the cottage had shifted something inside of him. Something about the curves of her hip, the angelic pout on her lips. Everything had called at him. Every sense of his being had come alive with need.

And the simple fool had no idea how close she had come to losing her virtue. No, it wasn't that they had almost kissed. No, it was because deep inside he knew that things would have gone much further.

The woman was too beautiful for him to have easily restrained himself. And he had seen it in her eyes. A burning need. If he had pressed his advantage, she would have surrendered everything. Of this there was no doubt in his mind at all.

He and Miss Isobel Stafford had come within seconds of ruining each other's lives all for a moment of pleasure.

Although, if he was honest with himself, it might very well have been worth it. The woman was intoxicating.

He was tempted to retrace his steps back to the cottage and take what she had unintentionally offered. Every part of his very soul called for it. Every thought was surrounded by pictures and feelings that tried to drive him back to her.

"No!"

Taking a deep breath, he forced himself to turn his back on the cottage and make his way through the orchard. But with each step he cursed himself for abandoning something that might have been the most important moment of his life.

Grinding his teeth, he passed through the orchard and up onto the main grounds just in time to see a carriage pull in before the main entrance.

His mother's guests, he realized. Arriving for their week of relaxation in the country.

"Typical," he mumbled to himself. Just what he needed. People he would have to be nice to. Of course, it might be a good thing. They would help keep his mind off of the woman he had just walked away from.

Sighing heavily, he began towards the carriage as First Lady Carlton and then Lady Burton exited the carriage. He watched as the young widow looked up at the house with an appraising eye. Then both women turned as a man stepped down from the carriage.

Brookenham frowned for a moment then scowled as he realized it was Lord Darlington.

A sick awareness filled him with anger. No, not him, not now.

Chapter Ten

"Lord Darlington is here, at the manor, Miss," Maggie said as she met her at the bedroom door.

"I know," Isobel answered as she hurried into the room to change. She did not want him to see her in a simple country frock.

Was this a sign? she wondered as she quickly slipped into her best day dress. She had only that morning decided that she must make a choice. And now, here he was.

As she wiggled into a different pair of slippers, she glanced out the window and sighed. She must honestly examine the facts before her. She desired a family. More than anything. To obtain one, she must marry. Love, true love, was not a requirement.

The one thing she knew without a doubt. The thought of being the pitied, maiden aunt was unthinkable.

The thought of her sisters made her ache inside. They had both found true love. Strong, kind men. Men who adored them for who they were, not what benefits they brought to the arrangement.

Nodding to herself, she gritted her teeth. If Darlington asked for her hand, she would accept.

The thought did not fill her with happiness but it did provide a small amount of contentment.

The decision had been made. They would pair well together. And he would father her children.

"I had not heard that Lord Darlington would be attending," Maggie said as she tucked at Isobel's hair.

"No," Isobel said with a shrug. "Lady Burton asked him to come along. Lady Brookenham says it is not unusual for extra guests to arrive at these type of things."

Maggie shook her head, obviously unable to understand the rules of the aristocracy. Isobel smiled to herself, like her maid, she would never completely understand these people. They saw the world through a prism of privilege. With a firm belief that a member of their class would always be accepted. At least as long as they continued to observe the rules and expectations of the class.

Had he come all this way because of her? The thought made her smile slightly. It was obvious that he and Brookenham did not enjoy each other's company. So, it must have been because of her.

That. Or he wished to spend time with Lady Burton, she thought with a sour stomach.

No, Lady Burton was the widow of a rich Earl. Darlington's estates were rather poor and his name not that illustrative. Isobel shook her head, Lady Burton accepting an offer from Lord Darlington would be a step down for her.

The thought created an uncomfortable feeling inside as Isobel left her room to join the guests in the main room. She must be realistic about these matters. Lord Darlington had set his sights on her because of the dowry offered by Norwich.

It made perfect sense from his perspective. An opportunity to become wealthy. Connection to two powerful Dukes. A mother for his heir. Yes, it made perfect sense. Somehow though, the realization did not sit well.

"Stop it," she whispered to herself. She must accept the reality of the situation and grow to live with it.

Wesley gave her a small smile as he opened the door to the main room and announced, "Miss Stafford, My Lady."

Isobel stepped into the room and hesitated. This was the room used for balls. The removable walls were in place making this part of the room more of a parlor. The next time his lordship held a large party, the walls would be removed and the room made into a large ballroom.

More people had arrived, she realized. At least a dozen in total. Would they have rooms for them all? Perhaps she and Aunt Ester should retire to the cottage after all.

Swallowing hard, she curtsied to Lady Brookenham then allowed the Countess to introduce her to her guests. Luckily, she knew almost everyone there. After three seasons in London, she had met almost every member of the ton.

What is more. They knew her. The young ward of the Duke of Norwich. While she might be a commoner, she had been admitted into their circle. Accepted as one of them. Yet she could feel the slight standoffishness. She was one of them, but barely.

As she exchanged pleasantries, she caught sight of Lord Brookenham in the corner, a whiskey in his hand. The man did not look pleased. She had to hold back a smile. He looked positively perturbed. This was so not how he preferred to spend his time. Entertaining people he barely knew and could care less for.

A memory of that morning's incident at the cottage flashed through her mind. Their eyes locked and she wondered if he was remembering how close they had come to a kiss. A sense of loss and regret filled her.

"Ah, Miss Stafford," a familiar voice called from behind her.

Before she turned to greet Lord Darlington, she caught Lord Brookenham's frown turn into a full-on scowl. The kind of scowl that would have terrified most people.

Taking a deep breath, she put on her best smile and turned to meet the Viscount of Darlington. As she curtsied, he bowed at the waist to kiss the back of her hand. His lips actually brushed against her skin, sending a small tingle up her arm as he looked down at her, giving her a knowing smile.

Her insides clenched with worry. Was she doing the right thing? She would never know, she realized. Not for years perhaps.

"Lord Darlington," she said. "I am so pleased to see you."

The blond Lord smiled back at her. His attention focused fully on her as if she were the most important thing in his life.

Isobel held her breath. Would he give her any hint of his intentions?

Still holding her hand, he stared into her eyes and said, "I felt drawn to the country. Something about the beauty pulled at me. I could not stay away."

Isobel's heart jumped. He was here because of her. She sighed internally. So, this was to be her husband? How interesting.

As he released her hand, Isobel glanced around the room and noticed that several of the women in the crowd were watching them closely. What were they thinking? she wondered. Was it obvious to them?

"How is your aunt?" the man asked.

"She is doing well, My Lord," Isobel answered.

He smiled at her then reached and took a cake from a passing footman. Isobel's stomach tightened when she realized that Lord Darlington didn't even acknowledge the man's presence. Never even so much as a thank you.

She frowned as a dozen thoughts jumped into her head. No, she told herself. It was not a disqualifying fault. Many people of the aristocracy treated their servants as no more important than the furniture. As if it was their due. Almost as if they were above such things as common courtesies.

It would be a goal of hers she thought. To help Lord Darlington see the error of his ways. Subtle suggestions and she was sure that she could expand his awareness of such matters.

"So, Darlington," Lord Brookenham said as he stepped away from his corner and joined them. "I never knew you enjoyed the country life. From what I have seen over the years, you are rarely in residence at your estates. Sorry, correction, estate. You have just the small one, I believe."

Isobel frowned at Lord Brookenham. Why was he being rude? Now of all times. Didn't he realize how important this was?

Lord Darlington frowned back at Lord Brookenham with a shrug then glanced back at her and said, "Some parts of the countryside are more interesting than others."

Brookenham scoffed and stared down at Isobel for a moment then shook his head and left.

What was that all about? she wondered. It was not like him to be rude. Normally, Lord Brookenham was kind to everyone. Well, everyone but her. They had fought too many times over the years for Isobel not to have seen this side of him, but normally it was only directed at her.

"I say," Lord Darlington said as he once again turned his full attention on her. "I have been told there is to be a dance tomorrow night. I am led to believe that several of the locals will also be attending. It does sound like fun. Don't you think?"

Isobel could only nod. She had known about the upcoming dance since shortly after her arrival. The Lord of the manor held one every year at about this time. Everyone would be there. She could remember attending with Ann and Lydia when she was younger.

This would be her first time as a member of the aristocracy. Her stomach tumbled. How would people treat her? Friends, acquaintances. She had been one of them at one time. Now she would be considered an outsider.

Would she always be the outsider? she wondered.

And what of Lord Darlington and his friends? What would they think of the villagers? Suddenly her stomach clenched up into a tight ball. Would they look down on them? Think them quaint, provincial.

The thought sent a bolt of fear straight to her heart. Lord Darlington would laugh at her village friends. And her village friends would take offense and blame her. Thinking she had become one them. A snob of the higher class.

Perhaps she should avoid the entire ordeal by claiming Aunt Ester needed her.

No, she realized as she looked up at Lord Darlington. Something in his eyes told her that he was going to ask her to marry him at the dance.

Her insides grew queasy.

"Excuse me, My Lord," she said quickly. "I need to return to my Aunt. I only came down to meet everyone."

His eyes grew cross for a moment then the hidden anger was quickly replaced by a smile that appeared slight forced.

"Of course, Miss Stafford," Lord Darlington said with a dip of his head. "I understand perfectly. Until later then. I do believe it will be most momentous."

Isobel swallowed hard as she curtsied and made a quick exit from the room. As she hurried up the stairs a sense of doubt filled her. Was she making the right decision? How could she know? But what choice did she have?

.oOo.

Lord Brookenham frowned as he watched Isobel scurry up the stairs. What was that all about? he wondered. Had that cad done something to upset her? No, surely not. Isobel was not the type of girl to take easy offense.

Besides, she was more likely to punch the scoundrel than run away in fear.

No, something else was bothering her. He could see it in the set of her shoulders, the furrowed brow. Deep in his gut, he could tell that things were not well for her.

Was it Darlington? Was he troubling her? Had the man proposed? Was that it? If so, why had that upset her? And why couldn't the woman see the scoundrel for who he was?

Arriving like this, uninvited. To a home where he was not wanted. What kind of man does that?

Lord Darlington walked around as if the world owed him everything. The way he held his head, the way he ignored everyone beneath him and curried favor with every one of higher status. Why couldn't she see him for his true self?

Growling under his breath he turned away. she must be allowed to lead her own life. Heaven knew she would never take any advice from him.

Suddenly, a ride sounded wonderful. An opportunity to get away from these people and think.

Sighing, he glanced up when he heard her door shut behind her.

"Isobel, Isobel," he muttered under his breath. "You are going to make a terrible mistake. And I can't do a thing to stop you."

Letting out a long breath, he shook his head. The world would work so much better if people just listened to him.

Chapter Eleven

The last note of music rang through the room as Isobel curtsied and Lord Darling bowed.

"Meet me in the library," he whispered as he leaned forward. "There is a matter I wish to discuss with you."

Her heart lurched. This was it. He was going to propose. She smiled softly and nodded.

Lord Darlington gave her hand a quick squeeze, then turned and left the room.

Isobel took a deep breath as she fought to calm her racing heart. This was the moment that her life would change forever. She would be Lady Darlington. Mother, Wife, Viscountess. Why was she not more thrilled? she wondered. Why were there no butterflies taking flight in her stomach?

The library? Wouldn't the gardens have been more romantic?

Because it is to be a business arrangement, she thought to herself. He gets a wealthy dowry, she a husband and father for her children.

Lifting her fan to hide the excitement in her eyes, she took a deep breath and wove her way through the crowd. She needed to be careful that she did not appear to be chasing after him. No, a simple turn about the room then she would step out into the hall.

As she nodded to Lady Wheaton, Isobel saw Lord Brookenham staring at her with a heavy scowl.

Why did he always look so upset? she wondered. He had not appeared that way at the cottage. He had seemed almost acceptably pleasant there. But since that moment, he had been like a bear with a thorn in his paw.

Ignoring him, she stepped out into the hall, looking both ways to ensure she was unobserved. Seeing that she was alone, she walked briskly to the library. Her heart continued to pound. Not with any romantic sentiment. No, just with the desire to finally have her path mapped out. To know her future.

Opening the door to the library, she saw the empty room and sighed with disappointment. She would be forced to wait a small while longer. Where was he?

The thought had no sooner entered her mind that the door opened behind her and Lord Darlington stepped into the room. He looked down at her with a kind smile. His blue eyes focused solely on her.

"Miss Stafford," he said as he took both of her hands.

Her stomach clenched up. He had closed the door behind him. The two of them were alone in this room, unchaperoned. What would Lady Brookenham say if she knew? Or The

Dowager? The woman would shake her head in disappointment.

It doesn't matter, she realized. She would shortly be betrothed. Almost all indiscretions could be forgiven if a young woman was engaged to be married.

"You look particularly beautiful tonight," Lord Darlington said as he stared down into her eyes.

Isobel smiled back. It was well that he found her attractive. It would make for an easier life together.

He paused for a moment then said, "As you know, I have always found you intriguing, and a delightful companion."

"And I you," she responded as she silently clenched her teeth. Hurry, she thought.

He smiled and nodded. "That is good because I believe we would get on well together. And would consider myself amongst the luckiest of men if you would agree to be my wife."

Isobel held her breath for a long moment. There finally.

"Lord Darlington," she began, but then hesitated. "I …"

The words would not come. What was wrong with her? Why couldn't she simply accept the man's offer?

The loud tick of the clock on the mantel drove home the awkwardness of the moment.

Slowly, his brow began to crease into an angry scowl.

"Lord Darlington," she said again, hoping if she began at the beginning, this time, the words would come.

The two of them stood there.

"Lord Darlington," she said for the third time. "I cannot." The words came out before she realized she was going to say them. But they were the truth, she realized. She could not marry this man. Something refused to allow her to say the words she needed to say.

"Why not?" he growled as his fingers squeezed hers enough to be uncomfortable.

"I am sorry My Lord, But I ..."

"How dare you," he interrupted. "How dare you deny me. You are nothing more than a ..."

Before he could finish his statement, the door opened behind him.

Something registered in his eyes as he sprang forward and pulled her into a tight embrace, his lips crushing hers. His hands roaming over her body.

Isobel was in shock as a dozen different emotions flashed through her. She had just rejected this man's proposal. And now he was mauling her as if she were a White Chapple strumpet.

"Oh, I do apologize," a high feminine voice said from the doorway.

Isobel pushed away enough from Lord Darlington to see Lady Burton studying them with a knowing smile. Her stomach fell as she realized what the woman would think. What everyone would think.

"My Lord," Isobel said as she managed to extricate herself from his grasp.

He stepped back with a knowing smile. A smirk really. He reminded her of a little boy who had gotten away with a cruel trick.

"It appears, Miss Stafford, that you no longer have a choice in the matter."

A sick, sour feeling filled her as she realized what had happened. Had he arranged this? Just in case she had refused him. Had he compromised her intentionally? He and Lady Burton were friends. Had he told her to follow them and discover them in a compromising position.

"Lord Darlington," she said. "Why would you wish to marry a woman who has refused you?"

He shrugged, "Your dowry will more than soothe my wounded pride."

Isobel gasped. To hear it put so bluntly drove home the fact that her instincts had been right. She could not marry this man. His cold, almost evil glare sent a shiver down her spine.

"As I said," the Viscount said with an evil smile. "You will marry me or no one. After this, no man of any standing will have you for his wife."

Her heart squeezed tight as the truth of his words sunk in. No man inside the ton would have her once she was compromised. No matter how much money Lord Norwich offered for her dowry. She would live out her life, alone in some country cottage. Cast aside like used baggage.

Even worse, her family would be shamed.

"Really, Sir, ..." she began but was lost for words. How could she extricate herself from this? How could she escape? Her mind frantically searched for a solution, but nothing presented itself.

"I must return to the party," he said with a knowing smile. "I will give you a moment to compose yourself. Then when you join me, I will make an announcement. Of course, I will discuss it with Norwich at a later date. But he will approve. Especially after he learns all of the details."

She sighed as her shoulders slumped in defeat. He was right. What choice did she have? It was this or a life of shame.

Turning, he walked to the door and reached for the doorknob then stopped and glanced back at her. "A few minutes, Isobel, that is all. Then I will expect you by my side."

She couldn't look at him as her world came apart around her. How was this possible? Earlier that day she had hoped he would ask her to marry him. Yet now, her dreams were being turned into a nightmare.

It would be a cold, lonely marriage. But he was right, what choice did she have?

Pacing back and forth, she tried to come up with a solution, but nothing occurred to her. It wasn't the thought of marriage that bothered her. It was to this man, especially now. To know that their life together had been manipulated and contrived made her shudder with anger.

Her head hung down as she walked back and forth trying to gather the courage to join him. To face all of those people and pretend that this was what she wanted.

The door opening surprised her. Had Darlington returned, upset that she had not joined him?

Lord Brookenham stormed into the room with an angry scowl that looked like he wanted to strangle something to death.

"What have you done?" he exclaimed.

"Me?" she asked as she turned on him, pleased to finally have something to yell at.

"There is a rumor spreading that you were found with Lord Darlington. Alone. That you enticed him into this room and seduced him into compromising you."

"What?" Isobel exclaimed. "And you believe that?"

Lord Brookenham studied her for a long moment then shook his head. Isobel could see his jaw tighten. He was fighting to maintain control.

"What happened?" he asked with a softness that surprised her.

Isobel hesitated for a moment. "We were alone. Together."

"Why?" he demanded. "How could you allow that to happen. Especially with that man of all men. You know the rules."

She sighed. "I believed he was going to ask me to marry him."

The Earl froze for a moment then asked, "Did he?"

Isobel held her breath for a moment then nodded. "But I declined him."

A deep frown creased his brow as he shook his head. "If you were going to decline him, why did you ever allow yourself to be alone with him?"

"I didn't know I was going to say no. It just came out. I didn't know that Lady Burton would find us. I didn't know he would pull me into an embrace just as she came in."

Lord Brookenham looked down at her as if she were a stupid child. How could she have been so naive? How had she let this happen?

He studied her for a long moment. "You do not wish to marry this man, is this correct? Why?"

She shrugged her shoulders. Why were they discussing this now? The reason why wasn't important. What was important was that she was going to have to marry a man she was beginning to despise.

"Why, Isobel?" the Earl insisted. "Is it the thought of being married to a man you don't love. Or is it this man in particular?"

She continued to look at him as she fought to find an answer.

"It is important," he said softly.

"It is him," she said as she let out a long breath. "I don't know why, but there was something that told me to say no, and I did so before I could stop myself. But once I did, I knew it was the right choice. Of course, it doesn't matter now. I will have to marry him."

The Earl squinted at her as he took a deep breath then let his shoulders slump in defeat.

"Come on," he said as he took her hand to lead her from the room.

She sighed heavily. Her life was ruined. She knew in the depths of her soul that she would never come to love Lord Darlington. Not after all of this. No, she would always feel like a used object.

But, as her intended had said, what choice did she   have?

Chapter Twelve

Brookenham fought to keep the anger boiling inside of him from exploding. This was not right. Isobel was being forced into a marriage she did not desire to a man beneath contempt.

Should he challenge him to a duel? Or better yet, simply beat the man to a ragged pulp? No, he couldn't kill the man, it would make things worse. Ruin Isobel and achieve nothing except to make him feel better.

Taking her hand, he slipped it into his arm and led her from the library. The sooner they got this over with, the better.

As they stepped into the ballroom. Every person turned to stare at them. Several of the women snickered and whispered behind their hands. Others frowned at her as if she had confirmed their worse thoughts.

He could feel Isobel tense up at the obvious disapproval in their eyes.

Across the room. Lord Darlington was talking to Lady Burton. The two of them obviously celebrating the success of their plans. Darlington froze for a moment, then smiled with satisfaction. Like a cat who had caught a mouse.

Brookenham decided at that moment that he would spend the rest of his days making this man's life intolerable.

"May I have your attention?" Brookenham called out, which was obviously unnecessary, as every face was focused on them already. "I have an announcement to make."

Isobel stared at the floor, ashamed, unable to meet the crowd's stares.

"I wish to inform you," he began. "That Miss Isobel Stafford has agreed to be my wife."

A gasp went up from the room. He quickly squeezed Isobel's hand to stop her from overreacting. But this was the only solution.

"You are all invited to the wedding of course," he added as he stared at Lord Darlington. There, you bastard. Your plans are ruined. Isobel might be forced to marry a man she didn't want. But at least he would not be a scoundrel.

Isobel stared up at him, her face as white as a sheet. "My Lord ..." she began.

"We will talk about it later," he whispered as he turned to receive the congratulations of the guests around them.

Lady Wheaton was the first to hurry forward. But, behind her, he saw his mother's face drawn with disapproval and despair. Like Isobel, he would deal with her later. Now he needed to get through the next few minutes before things got out of control.

Smiling at Lady Wheaton, he accepted her congratulations then leaned forward and whispered. "Don't tell anyone, but Isobel and I have been discussing this for years."

Lady Wheaton's eyes widened in surprise as she looked at Isobel for confirmation. Isobel smiled weakly and nodded. Lady Wheaton frowned for a second, then turned to look back at Lord Darlington.

"But I thought …" the Baroness began.

Brookenham raised a single eyebrow, daring her to say anything that might bring shame on his betrothed.

The woman wisely held her tongue. That was one of the benefits of being a powerful Earl. People feared upsetting him.

He kept an eye on Isobel as the others came forward to offer their congratulations. Her face was as white as a summer cloud and her brow remained furrowed in confusion. His heart went out to her. This was not her fault. No, that could be laid at the feet of that bastard Darlington.

"Brookenham?" his mother said with a questioning look.

He smiled down at his mother and shook his head slightly. Not here, he silently told her.

She sighed heavily then turned to take Isobel's hands. "Welcome to the family, My Dear."

Isobel blushed then curtsied, "Thank you, My Lady."

Seeing that the things were going to become too emotional, Brookenham nodded to the musicians and said, "A waltz."

As the musicians prepared themselves, he turned to Isobel and raised an eyebrow. "May I have this dance, My Dear?"

Isobel balked for a second then meekly nodded, obviously still dazed by the turn of events. He needed to get her alone to explain. But before they could escape they needed to lay the foundation that everything was perfectly fine between them. That all proprieties had been met.

Taking her hand, he led her out to the floor. His heart jumped just a little as he realized this would be their first time dancing a waltz together.

As his arm slipped around her waist, a sense of rightness filled him. The woman was beautiful, of that there was no doubt, but the knowledge that she would be his wife. His responsibility, his to protect, gave him a sense of possessiveness. A sense of meaning almost.

When the music began, the other couples remained to the side. Giving them the entire floor. It was as if by some unspoken agreement, all of the guests had chosen to give them this one moment alone.

"Why?" Isobel asked as she stared up at him.

She danced well, he realized as he fought to develop an answer.

"Because I couldn't abide the thought of that man getting away with it."

She frowned then looked down, unable to hold his stare.

"I am sorry," she said so softly that he barely heard her.

"We will make it work," he replied as a sudden doubt filled him. What had he done? He and this woman were to be wed. He had been good and well caught. What was worse, he had chosen to be trapped.

Sighing, he bit the inside of his mouth to stop from telling her his true thoughts. It was not her fault he reminded himself. He should strive to never make her feel guilty for taking away his freedom.

No. Not if they were to make this work.

.oOo.

Isobel's mind whirled in a thousand different directions as Lord Brookenham led her around the dance floor. The feel of his arm around her waist felt both comforting and possessive. As if he were protecting her from the evils of this world.

And that was what he had done, she realized. By stepping in, he had rescued her from Lord Darlington. Just as he had rescued her in the alley after her visit to the museum.

No. she could not allow this. He shouldn't have to sacrifice himself for her.

The thought sent a sense of fear to her very soul. How is she going to get out of this without ruining her life? Or worse, his?

Why had he done it? When she had asked, he had simply said it was to defeat Lord Darlington. Was that all it was? Some manly competition between the two of them that would not allow Brookenham to accept Lord Darlington succeeding?

Surely not. Surely Lord Brookenham would not sacrifice his entire future happiness for such a silly reason.

Glancing up at him she swallowed hard as she realized that the man might very well do such a stupid thing. It was exactly the type of idiotic action that Lord Brookenham would do. The man was a hero at heart. Always rushing in to save others. He didn't have the good sense God gave him.

Biting her lip, she stopped herself from calling him an idiot. Instead, she said, "My Lord. I believe we need to discuss things."

He laughed, "Do you think so?"

She frowned up at him and shook her head, how could he tease her at a time like this.

"I suggest the garden," he said with a smirk. "It is so much more romantic for newly betrothed. Don't you think?"

Her heart shivered as she nodded her acceptance.

Swirling her in a last turn, he pulled back, bowed, then held out his arm for her.

Isobel fought to catch her breath, then placed her hand on his arm and let him lead her out of the room. As she walked, every eye in the room focused on them alone. Staring with curiosity and judgment. She made sure to keep her head high, under no circumstances would she let them think she was terrified.

Once they had stepped out into the cool night air, Isobel faltered for a moment as the soft scent of roses washed over her.

"This way, My Dear," Brookenham said to her as he took her elbow and guided her down the steps into the garden.

Isobel nervously glanced over her shoulder. They were leaving the party unescorted.

"Do not worry, My Dear," he said with a knowing smile. "We will stay in sight of the guests. I would wager that even now my mother is watching us closely. Besides, now that we are engaged, certain liberties will be allowed."

She sighed. "I do not believe your mother was pleased with your announcement."

He shrugged his wide shoulders, obviously letting her know that his mother's concerns were not his.

"Her wishes might not concern you," Isobel said as she stepped away from him to give her some room. Being too close confused her mind she was coming to realize. "But it is very much a concern of mine," she added. "I do not wish to upset my future mother-in-law."

Again, he shrugged as he studied her. Suddenly, she realized that this man was to be her husband. They would be sharing a life together. Her and Brookenham. No, it was even more, they would be sharing a bed together.

The thought made her face grow warm. She turned away so that he wouldn't see, but was not fast enough.

He gently pulled her back. "We will make it work."

She frowned, "You keep saying that. How? We can barely stand each other."

Again, he shrugged. It really was becoming rather disturbing. Nothing seemed to impact this man. Troubles seemed to roll off him like a wind over rocks.

That was him, she realized. He was a rock. A solid force of nature. Nothing stopped him. Not brigands in alleyways. Not despicable Lords at a country dance. Her heart jumped as she realized what he had sacrificed for her.

"You never wished to marry," she said as she fought to understand.

Again, with that damn shrug. "Things change."

"My Lord ..." she began.

"James," he said as he held her shoulders. "At least when we are alone."

She gawked up at him. His words had driven home how real this was. He wasn't going to back out. He wasn't going to pretend that it hadn't happened, No, he was intending to go through with it.

"James," she said.

He smiled and nodded for her to continue. "I know it is unusual for a wife of a Lord to call her husband by his given name. But I prefer it. Probably because I never expected to be a Lord."

Isobel fought to remember what she was going to say. But it had become lost in the back of her brain somewhere.

"And I will be a Countess," she said with disbelief as the new realization settled over her.

"A wealthy Countess at that," he added with a smile.

Isobel could only shake her head. How was this possible?

"What of Norwich? What if he refuses his permission?" she asked.

He frowned slightly and scoffed. "I would think Norwich would be pleased to be rid of you," he said with a teasing smile.

She hit him in the shoulder before she remembered that there were over a dozen people watching them.

"I am sorry My Lord."

He laughed. "No, it is I who should apologize. I shouldn't tease you that way. Believe me, Norwich will not be a problem. Neither will my mother. I assure you."

Isobel took a deep breath as she looked up at him. This man was to be her husband. The thought continued to devil her. To rush in and out of her brain as she fought to hold onto it.

"I will obtain a special license. The Bishop is a good friend. We will be married the day after tomorrow."

"So quickly?" she gasped.

Again, he shrugged. "It is for the best. It will halt any rumors before they can begin."

She sighed heavily as she nodded her acceptance. "I must get word to Ann and Lydia. They will be so upset to miss my wedding."

"It is for the best," he told her. "I would prefer our guests returned to London with us already wed."

She looked up at him. "You just want to upset Darlington."

He laughed. "The man is lucky I don't put a bullet through his skull. Watching you marry another man will have to be punishment enough. Knowing that I do not need your dowry will make it even worse."

Isobel frowned. This was not how she had dreamed of her wedding. But, Lord Brookenham was correct. It was best to stop rumors before they could begin. She knew very well that people would talk, but if she and the Earl were married, the stories would not go far.

Of course, Ann and Lydia would be hurt. But if she explained it carefully, they would understand eventually.

"Very well," she said to him. "We will be married the day after tomorrow."

He smiled down at her and then said, "And once we are wed, I will send them on their way. Along with my mother. I refuse to share my wedding night with a house full of guests."

Her cheeks erupted in heat. Suddenly, marriage and all of its ramifications seemed too   real.

Chapter Thirteen

"What were you thinking?" his mother said to him through gritted teeth.

Lord Brookenham smiled over her head at the crowded room, ignoring her for a moment, then leaned forward and said in a low voice, "You were the one pushing me to marry."

"The daughter of a Duke, an Earl at least. Not ..."

"Careful mother, that is my betrothed you are talking about."

The Countess Brookenham bit her lip. Lord Brookenham almost smiled. The thought of upsetting his mother over this matter had become an unexpected benefit. The woman had hounded and prodded him for years. Now, once he had finally given her what she wanted, she complained. So typical.

Taking a deep breath, the older woman tried again. "Is it really necessary? Surely Darlington would make an excellent match for Isobel. She isn't even a Lady."

Brookenham shook his head, he had always known of his mother's prejudices, but to see them so prominently displayed was troubling.

"Regardless, Mother, Isobel is to be my Countess and you must come to accept it."

"And if I don't," she said as she stood up straight and stared up at him then quickly looked around to see if anyone had heard her.

He laughed. "Then, The dowager house and a small allowance will have to be compensation. Of course, you will be allowed to visit with the grandchildren on your birthday."

Her face grew pale as the threat took hold. He continued to stare at her, ensuring she understood just how serious he was.

"You will be nice to Isobel," he continued. "You will help her in any way you can. If so, I will allow you to remain a part of our family."

"James," she gasped as she stared up at him as if she had never seen this facet of him before.

He continued to stare into her eyes until she, at last, slumped in defeat and nodded her head. "Very well, I see that I cannot sway you on this matter."

"No. Mother, You can't."

"You don't even care for the girl. Really, why do this?

"I could say it is because of a sense of honor. Or, a duty to Norwich. It doesn't matter though. It is going to happen."

"But two days to arrange a wedding. Surely, we can postpone. I had always wanted your wedding to be at St. Paul's."

"No." he replied. "Two days, then everyone back to London. If they are going to spread stories let them be about the wedding."

She continued to look up at him, "You always were a stubborn child."

He laughed, "I got it from you."

Lady Brookenham smiled slightly then sighed. "Two days. It will take a miracle."

"I believe you can do it mother."

His mother sighed again then nodded, accepting the challenge.

The wedding was the least of his problems, he realized. No, it was the marriage itself that concerned him. How were he and Isobel ever to exist together?

Thankfully. England was large enough. They need rarely interact. He would have to live in London. His duties in Parliament would demand it. But she could remain here on the estate and have a perfectly fine life.

For some reason, the thought was not as acceptable as he would have preferred. But it was probably for the best.

.oOo.

Isobel's head floated in a cloud of confusion. How had this happened? What were her sisters going to say when they found out? What of her friends? The people she knew?

Everyone would think she had trapped Lord Brookenham. That she had somehow connived and fooled the Earl. Of course, anyone who knew the man would find the idea preposterous. He wasn't the type of man who could be pushed into something against his will.

No. She had only unintentionally set it up so that he must rescue her. The one thing he could not resist. Or, at least that was what it would look like to everyone she knew.

"I must say, Miss Stafford," Lady Burton said as she approached. The look in her eyes and the tilt of her head led Isobel to believe the woman was upset.

"I am impressed." She continued. "To have both a Viscount and an Earl fighting over you. Well done."

Isobel's stomach clenched tight as she turned to greet the woman. This was the person who had worked with Lord Darlington, she reminded herself. Be careful. She does not have your best interest at heart.

"It was not as it appears," she responded. "Neither of them were fighting over me. I assure you."

Lady Burton raised an eyebrow in doubt. "Really? From where I stand, it appears that you used Lord Darlington to bring Brookenham to the mark. Well played, my dear My Dear. Very well played."

"It wasn't ... never mind," Isobel said with a shake of her head. She would never be able to convince this woman or anyone else for that matter that the results had not been her intention.

"Have you seen Lord Darlington?" Isobel asked. She needed to talk to him. To apologize. This was all her fault. She had led the man to believe she would be agreeable to his offer.

Lady Burton shook her head. "I believe he has borrowed one of the Earl's horses and is on his way back to London. But then, you can't really blame the man, can you? You didn't really expect him to stay for the wedding, surely."

Isobel's stomach fell. One more thing for her to be ashamed about. Would this day ever end?

She frantically tried to think of some way to change the conversation. Luckily, Lady Brookenham chose that moment to join them.

"Lady Burton," the older woman said with a false smile as she approached. "Will you excuse us for a moment. My future daughter-in-law and I have much to discuss."

A shiver of fear traveled down Isobel's spine. She had been dreading this confrontation since the moment Brookenham had made his announcement.

"Of course," Lady Burton said, shooting Isobel a quick smile of satisfaction. It was obvious that Lady Brookenham was about to express her displeasure about the entire situation. And anything that caused Isobel distress was to be encouraged.

Isobel held her breath as both of them watched Lady Burton make her way across the room to join Lady Wheaton and Lady Sheffield.

"I do not like that woman," Lady Brookenham said with a shake of her head. "Whatever you do. Never trust her with a secret."

Isobel's eyes grew wide, surprised to find the Countess taking her side.

"Now then," Lady Brookenham said as she slipped her arm into Isobel's and started to lead her from the room. "Let us find a private location so we can discuss things without everyone and their sister commenting."

Isobel reluctantly nodded as she let herself be led from the room. This could not be avoided. This woman was to be part of her life. Steeling herself to the inevitable, Isobel set her jaw and followed the Countess across the hall and into the library.

Had she chosen this room on purpose? Isobel wondered as she fought to maintain her courage.

The Countess turned and slowly examined her. The woman's eyes traveled up and down as is she was inspecting a bolt of cloth.

"I can't say that I am pleased about this marriage," the Countess began.

Isobel swallowed hard. That was blunt. Even for the Earl's mother.

"I have known you and your sisters for years," the older woman continued. "I had hoped for someone of higher status for my son. Our side of the family had only recently come to the title. I hoped a good match would solidify our standing in the ton."

A sense of shame washed through Isobel. Of course, she wasn't good enough for the Earl. She was nothing more than a country miss. Her family had been a tenant of his, for heaven sake. She had not been born to this life.

"But," the older woman continued, "we must make the best of a bad situation."

Isobel winced, that was what she was to this woman. A bad situation. But then how could she blame her? She was a mother who cared for her son. It must hurt her enormously to see him married to a woman he didn't love. A woman who brought nothing to the marriage. Neither status nor wealth.

"My Lady," Isobel began. "I can assure this was not my plan. I was surprised as yourself when Lord Brookenham made his announcement."

The Countess nodded. "I believe you. But that does not change the fact that you have not been trained for this life."

Taken aback, Isobel frowned. "My Lady, I can assure that I have had expert examples in my sisters. They have both become well respected Duchesses, surely even you can admit to that."

The Countess nodded. "Yes, but those were marriages founded in love."

Isobel almost snorted. If the Countess only knew the truth. Both had started out as a result of errors, but they had both grown into love matches.

Could such a thing happen here? she wondered as a bolt of excitement shot through her. Was there such a chance?

No, she realized. She and Brookenham knew each other too well. They had long ago passed the point where two people could fall in love.

No, this would be a marriage in name only. She would provide an heir or two, but otherwise, they would live separate lives. A sadness filled her, but she must never be bitter, she told herself. Brookenham had sacrificed himself for her. She must never forget that. Granted, her marriage would never be a fairy tale. But Brookenham was an honorable man. Perhaps that was all that she could ever hope for.

Lady Brookenham continued to watch her then sighed heavily. "Regardless of my feelings on the matter. You are to be married in two days Brookenham informs me. And he is adamant."

Isobel nodded as she swallowed hard. It was still difficult for her to wrap her thoughts around the idea of marrying Lord Brookenham at all, let alone in two days.

"So," Lady Brookenham continued, "I thought a simple wedding, here, in the main room. Our guests. Any friends from the village you would wish to invite. A reception immediately following. Two days should be enough time for Cook to prepare. With your permission, I will discuss a menu with her."

Once again, Isobel nodded as she fought to hold back the fear rising inside of her. This was real. This was inevitable. All this time, ever since the announcement, she had believed it was all a trick. A distant thought that would burst at any moment.

But no. this was real.

"And, after the reception," Lady Brookenham said, "His Lordship has insisted the guests and myself depart for London."

Isobel's cheeks erupted with warmth as she felt herself blush. Unable to meet the older woman's eyes, she focused on the ground beneath her feet.

"Yes, well," the Countess continued, "I will expect you have a dress and such. It will not be as fine as you wished, but then we are in a hurry. A light pastel, I should think. I don't hold with this new fashion of white for a wedding dress. It seems too much. I, of course, will coordinate the staff, cook, the Vicar, and all of the other details."

"Thank you," Isobel said with a heavy sigh. "I don't know how I would ever have been able to do it myself."

The Countess nodded. "Yes, well, you will need to pay attention. As this is the type of thing expected of a Countess, My Dear."

Isobel nodded, afraid if she said anything it would be the wrong thing. Perhaps she could just make everyone's life easier if she was to slink off to the continent for the next twenty years.

The Countess continued to stare at her for a long moment then sighed audibly. "James is my only remaining child. When his older brother, John, was killed in Portugal I thought I would never find happiness again. It was only because of James that I could even face another day."

"I know how important he is to you," Isobel said.

"Yes, well, you can repay me by giving me a great many grandchildren."

Isobel blushed as she realized what must be done to accomplish such a thing. She was tempted to ask a question or two about her wedding night. Something she would have asked of Ann. But then realized this was to be her mother-in-law and bit her tongue to stop herself.

"I look forward to having a family," she said instead.

But in the depth of her heart, Isobel knew that this was not the marriage this woman had wanted for her only son. And she would never be pleased about the matter. The best Isobel could hope for was an uneasy peace between them.

But then, the same could be said about the relationship with Lord Brookenham as well.

Chapter Fourteen

Maggie pulled the brush through Isobel's hair for the ninety-eighth time.

"A Countess," the maid said with a shake of her.

Isobel's stomach tightened once again. Today was her wedding day. Mere hours from now she realized. It could not be avoided. There was no escape. She and Lord Brookenham would become husband and wife. Both against their will.

How was this possible? They hadn't even discussed their future. Not really. She had barely seen the man since his shocking announcement. And now she was being rushed into a situation that felt wrong. It wasn't right.

"Do you think the Earl is in his study?" Isobel asked her maid.

"Either there or his rooms. But I saw Davies, his valet, downstairs in the kitchen working on a button of his Lordship's coat."

"Do you think he is alone?"

Again, the maid shrugged as she continued to brush Isobel's hair. "I imagine so. Most of the guests are not up and about yet. So yes, probably. Unless Wesley is with him. But I doubt it. The butler has too many things to see to today of all days."

Isobel nodded to herself. Yes, Lord Brookenham was probably down in his study this very moment, pacing back and forth as he desperately tried to discover a way out of this disaster.

"I must see him," Isobel said as she jumped up from the dressing table.

"Miss!" Maggie exclaimed as Isobel pulled the belt of her robe tight and shot her maid a quick smile.

Why must she follow the rules? Isobel thought to herself as she stuck her head out into the hall. What would they do to her? Make her get married to a man who didn't love her? No, it would be safe enough and besides, it was her wedding day. Brides were forgiven social errors on their wedding day.

Sneaking down the stairs one step at the time, her head shifted back and forth. The click of the door lock from below had her freezing in place until Betty, the downstairs maid crossed the hall and entered the main room.

Once she was positive the route was clear, Isobel scurried down the stairs and into the study without knocking.

Lord Brookenham's forehead creased into a dozen lines as he looked up from his desk.

"Isobel?" he asked, obviously surprised to see her.

Now that she was there, Isobel froze as she tried to remember why she had come.

Suddenly, it seemed foolish. Ridiculous to be seen in her robe, her hair only partly completed. But this was to be her husband. He would see so much more very soon. He would come to know everything about her. Every fault, every error.

"Is everything all right?" he asked as he stood up and came around to stand in front of his desk. He had not been pacing she realized. He wasn't desperately trying to find a way out. Why not?

"Of course, everything is not all right," she said with a heavy sigh. Turning she walked to the far end of the room and then back once again.

"And the problem is?" he asked as he leaned back to rest on his huge desk, folded his arms, and cocked an eyebrow.

She ground her teeth. Why didn't he seem as terrified as she felt?

"We ... You and I of all people, are to be married."

He laughed slightly. "And you thought it wise to come downstairs only half dressed to advise me of this fact. I do believe it was already on my schedule for the day. There was no need to inform me."

Isobel felt a tide of anger wash over her. "Lord Brookenham ..."

"James, remember when we are alone of course."

She continued to grit her teeth, "James. We can't be married. It will never work. We despise each other."

He winced backwards as if she had sliced at him with a knife. "Our feelings have little to do with the matter. It must be allowed to play itself out."

Isobel bit back the angry rebuke and turned to pace once again.

"Really Isobel, you must come to accept the inevitable. We will make it work."

"You keep saying that. How?"

He frowned at her for a long time then said, "Are you worried about the wedding night? Because, if so, we can forgo the entire thing."

She balked as she felt the blood drain from her face. Did he not want her? Was it such an insignificant event that it could be dismissed at a moment's notice?

She had always believed such things were important to men. If he did not care to go through with it. Did that mean he had another woman somewhere? Was that why?

He studied her for a moment then smiled softly and said, "I assure you, I wish to ... enjoy my new wife. Believe me. But I will not force you. I will not demand my husbandly rights."

A mistress, she realized, the man must have a mistress, either here in the village, or back in London. Or even more likely, both. Her mind immediately compiled a list of possible candidates. Both guests and villagers.

She felt her cheeks grow warm as the blood rushed back into her face. This was not what she had hoped to discuss, she thought. But immediately realized it really was at the heart of the matter.

Stopping her pacing, she pulled up in front of him and looked up into his eyes. He really is tall, she realized, with such wide shoulders and a handsome face. Not as pretty as Darlington, but larger, more male.

As she swallowed hard, she nodded slightly and said, "I desire a family. That was how I … we, got into this mess."

He studied her for a long second then smirked and nodded. "Of course."

Just two words, she thought. No comment. No teasing. Just an acceptance of her statement. Her stomach turned over with the realization that there really was no way out. Tonight, that very night, she would lay with this man. He would take her virginity. How could she do that with a man she did not love and who did not love her?

How was she to act? Simply lay there until he was done? They had never even kissed. And she was to allow him to do what he must if she was to have a baby. The thought sent a nervousness through her entire body.

Suddenly, she desperately wished to be anywhere but there.

"Excuse me, My Lord," she said as she turned and left the room before she could become even more embarrassed. Flying up the stairs she slammed the bedroom door behind her.

Maggie was brushing her wedding dress. Turning, she frowned and gave Isobel a puzzled look.

"Was His Lordship in the study?" the maid asked.

Isobel ignored her as she began to pace back and forth before the fireplace. There had to be a way out. A way to avoid this pending disaster. Her stomach turned over as she chewed at the inside of her cheek.

He didn't want her. That was rather obvious. His sense of duty had forced him into this awful situation. The man had actually said that he did not care if she shared his bed or not. How could he be so cold? So uncaring. It would be a hard, distant marriage she realized. Two people putting on a charade for the rest of society.

Even if they did eventually ... couple. It would be a cold, passionless coming together. The thought filled her with sadness as she looked out at the future. A long cold future.

.oOo.

Lord Brookenham bit back a heavy sigh. No need for Isobel to know how much he

148

regretted this situation. But it could no longer be avoided. The Vicar was saying the words. The room was filled with witnesses. No, he was participating in his own wedding. An occurrence he would have sworn would be impossible.

At least his wife was beautiful. If a man was to have a wife, it was better if she was pretty. And intelligent, he thought. That was another of Isobel's good points. The woman was as smart as a Cambridge Don. Of course, that could be a hindrance. That intellect was attached to a sharp tongue.

He almost shuddered when he thought of their future together. Would they spend their time scratching and poking at each other? Or, avoiding contact entirely? It was probably for the best if it was the latter.

"You may kiss the bride," the Vicar said, bringing Brookenham back to reality.

As he looked down at his wife, he caught a hint of fear behind her eyes. Why? he wondered. Wasn't this what she had wanted? A marriage, a family of her own. What did she have to fear? He was wealthy with an honorable family name. An Earl for heaven sake.

You would think the girl would be ecstatic. But no. All he saw was a hint of fear and trepidation.

This was his wife, he realized with a sudden weight. His to provide for and protect. His responsibility. A sudden possessiveness surprised him. His wife. Words he had always thought he would never utter.

As he stared down at her, that look of fear in her eyes slowly turned over to one of rising anger. A subtle cough from the crowd made him remember why his wife might be upset. He was to kiss her.

Well, there were worse ways to spend his time. She was beautiful, young, innocent, afraid, and angry all at once. A tantalizing combination, he was discovering.

"Lady Brookenham," he said with a soft smile as he cradled her face in his hands and slowly brought his mouth to hers. A sharp thrill flashed between them. Surprising both himself and Isobel.

She pulled back, her eyes as wide as saucers. He smiled again, then leaned forward and kissed her once more. Determined to finish what they had begun. Their lips caressed each other. Discovering. A man could grow to enjoy this, he realized. Kissing a beautiful woman, torn between curiosity and hidden passion, was surprisingly enticing.

Yes, most surprising.

At last, he forced himself to pull back. Looking deep into her eyes he could see the shock she was feeling and something else. Hope perhaps.

Swallowing hard, he mentally kicked himself for giving her the option to forgo the wedding night. Perhaps he had acted too hastily. He would never force her. But that did not mean he couldn't regret his offer.

Do not forget, he reminded himself. She said she had wanted children. Thankfully there was but one way to ensure that she became with child. A thought he found most pleasing.

Giving her one last smile, he placed her hand on his arm, then turned them both to meet the crowd of well-wishers.

As they looked out over the crowd, he glanced at Isobel to find her staring up at him with a strange look. As if her world was slightly off-kilter.

A vision of their coming time together flashed into his mind and he couldn't help himself from smiling with satisfaction. Isobel caught something in his expression and her cheeks flashed full red.

He couldn't stop himself from smiling even more as he realized just how appropriate the term 'Blushing Bride' had become. The woman was delectable. And she would be his, this very night.

The only thing that could have made it better would have been if Darlington had remained for the ceremony. Oh, how he wished to have seen the man's eyes when he realized just how much he had lost.

Glancing down at Isobel, he registered the fierce determination in her eyes. A sense of pride filled him. This was his Countess. One of the strongest women he had ever known. She would do well.

As both Lady Burton and Lady Wheaton talked over each other about how nice the ceremony was. About her dress, the flowers. And another dozen questions, Brookenham watched as Isobel handled them flawlessly, then smiled to himself. The woman needed to be teased.

Leaning down, he whispered, "Say the word and we can forgo the reception."

Isobel's brow furrowed in confusion as she turned to look at him. Then, the realization of what he was truly saying sank in and all color drained from her face.

He smirked, holding her stare for a long beat as he cocked an eyebrow.

Her cheeks flushed again as she shot him an evil stare, then turned back to their guests. But he had seen something deep inside of her stare. A brief spark of pleasure had fought with her desire to hit him.

Interesting, he thought. It appeared that his wife was not completely unaware of the potential between them.

Chapter Fifteen

Isobel gritted her teeth. It was as if every nerve was alight with pure terror. The guests were leaving. A long line of coaches was arranged in the main drive waiting for their passengers.

"Congratulations, again My Lady," Lady Wheaton said with a slight curtsey.

Isobel was tempted to look over her shoulder to see who Lady Wheaton was talking to. It happened every time someone called her My Lady. Would she ever become used to it?

"Thank you so much," Isobel told the older woman.

"Come, My Dear," Lord Wheaton said as one of the footmen opened the coach door. "Let us leave these young people alone. The last thing they need is a gaggle of ancients such as ourselves overstaying our welcome. They have more important things to attend to."

Isobel caught the wink that Baron shot Brookenham and her stomach clenched at the reminder of what was to come.

Lady Wheaton laughed at her husband's crude remark, then glanced at Lord Brookenham and sighed heavily. "You are a very fortunate young woman," the Baroness whispered to her with a slight shake of her head. "In more ways than you will ever know."

Isobel frowned but held her tongue as Lady Wheaton gave them both one last smile, then climbed up into the carriage. The Baron joined her then used his cane to tap the side of the carriage. The coachman yelled as he flicked the ribbons and the vehicle was away.

Next, her dear Aunt Ester stepped forward as she pulled a shawl around her shoulders. "You look beautiful," the older woman said for the seventh time that day.

Isobel sighed, today was one of her aunts confused days. She had moved back to the cottage the prior evening but Isobel still worried for her safety and happiness.

"I will come to visit tomorrow," Isobel said as she took her hands.

"Oh no dear," Aunt Ester said as she shook her head. "You will be too tired. No, a few days, then you must visit."

Isobel's stomach fell at the casual way her aunt treated the entire event. As if her niece were walking to the village and back.

Aunt Ester kissed her on the cheek then turned and left without another word. Without having to be told, Wesley shot a glance at one of the footmen who fell out of formation and hurried after the older woman to make sure she got back to the cottage safely.

Isobel's heart ached. At least she had one family member at the wedding.

"Well, Brookenham," his mother said as she stepped forward, pulling on her gloves. "I am off. Although, I must say, this is rather irregular. It is the young couple who should be departing not the wedding guests."

"I will expect you to manage the story of our nuptials, Mother," Lord Brookenham said. "Heaven knows you are an expert at such things."

Isobel flinched at the reminder of exactly how they had ended up in this situation.

London would be abuzz with rumor and shocked whispers. Was it true that the Earl had been trapped into a marriage? Others would say that he had caught his intended with another man and rushed the marriage before anyone could object.

Still, others would say it was Brookenham that had compromised her. That and a dozen variants of the story would spread through the city. It was Lady Brookenham's responsibility to stop the stories from getting out of hand.

"I will try," she said with a deep frown, then sighed as she turned to Isobel, she smiled with resignation. "He and his dictatorial ways are now your problem, My Dear," the older woman said as she leaned forward to kiss Isobel on the cheek. "Heaven knows I have tried and failed to make him realize that not everyone sees the world as he does."

Isobel froze for a brief second. Was she to agree with her mother-in-law or protect her husband's honor? Which was expected of her? Once again, she was reminded just how far from her normal world she had traveled in a single day.

Before she could say anything, the Earl laughed and shook his head. "Everything I know about being … in charge. I learned from you, Mother."

A sense of relief flashed through Isobel as she realized her husband did not need her help. But that didn't stop her from being surprised by a sense of possessiveness. He was her husband after all.

"I assure you, My Lady," Isobel said as she lifted her chin. "Lord Brookenham's … ways … can, at times, be very beneficial."

The older woman's brow furrowed as she snorted and shook her head. Then pulling Isobel to the side, she leaned forward to whisper, "There is so much you need to know …"

Isobel's stomach churned as a sudden fear filled her. Was Brookenham's mother going to give her advice about the wedding night? Here, in the drive, in front of her son? No, surely not.

"… be careful," The Dowager Countess said. "Cook is too fond of the sherry, and Wesley visits a woman in the next village every other Saturday. You must ignore this. Good butlers and good cooks are so hard to find. Footmen and maids can be replaced. But not a good cook."

Isobel gasped. Not in surprise so much. But in the fact that the Countess even knew about such things.

"Of course, My Lady," Isobel said as her mind whirled with the realization that the staff were now her concern. Hers to manage and oversee. How was this possible? She was only nineteen years old. How could she tell a dozen people what to do?

Brookenham waived off a footman as he opened the coach door and held out a hand to assist his mother.

"Have a pleasant trip," he said as he handed her up into the carriage.

As The Dowager Countess arranged her dress around her, she looked out the window at her son and shook her head. Isobel was surprised to see a tear in the corner of the older woman's eye. The woman started to say something then thought better of it and sat back and nodded.

Brookenham balked for just a moment then stepped back and nodded to the coachman.

As the two of them watched the coach pull away, Isobel felt an overwhelming sense of apprehension fill her with an aloneness. Even standing there next to Brookenham. It felt as if a connection with her old world had been broken.

This was the beginning of her new life, she realized. The two of them.

She glanced up and was surprised to see a bit of a sad expression on Brookenham's face.

"What are you thinking?" she asked before she could stop herself.

His expression immediately changed back to the normal nonchalance she was used to. But she raised an eyebrow, silently demanding to know the answer.

He shrugged and said, "I wished my brother was still alive. I do not believe my mother will ever know true happiness again. It was as if the day he died, her reason for living ended."

Isobel was shocked at his words. And realized that there was more to this man than was commonly known. There were layers that he kept hidden.

"Come, My Dear," he said as he took her arm. "We have a life to begin."

Her insides fell as she realized just how true his words were.

As they stepped back into the house, she was surprised to see the bustle and activity as the staff brought the house back into compliance with Wesley's strict expectations. The walls were being rehung. The clutter from the reception removed and the furniture being returned to its rightful place.

This was her home now she realized with a sudden shock as Wesley approached them then bowed at the waist. "My Lord, My Lady, we should have things back to their proper placement shortly."

Isobel felt an internal shock when she heard the butler call her Lady. Would she always feel this shock? she wondered. Or would she grow to become accustomed to it? One thing she knew deep in her heart. She would never grow to expect it.

What was she supposed to say? Was she expected to take charge, issue instructions? No, surely not. Wesley knew more about such matters than she ever would. So, what was her responsibility?

Suddenly, the thought of being a Countess seemed to be a mountain too large to ever be climbed.

"Why don't we step into the library and out of their way,?" Brookenham said as he pointed to the room in question.

Isobel sighed, once again saved by Brookenham. He was giving her an escape.

As he held the door for her, she took a deep breath and caught a hint of his sandalwood cologne. Before she could bask in the masculine aroma, the Earl closed the door behind them and smiled softly before he went to his desk and started rifling through his papers.

Isobel looked around the room then at her husband behind his desk.

"What now?" she asked.

He looked up and smiled slowly. "It is our wedding day, My Dear. Surely, you have learned about such things."

Her cheeks erupted with heat but she refused to look down with embarrassment.

"I mean, what are my duties as a Countess?"

The Earl studied her for a moment then shrugged his shoulders. "Honestly, I don't know exactly. Don't forget, I didn't grow up the son of an Earl. I never exactly paid attention to such matters. My mother didn't talk with you?"

Isobel felt her stomach clench up with fear as she shook her head.

He frowned then shrugged. "I suppose it doesn't really matter. After all. I am the only one you must concern yourself with."

Isobel snorted with derision before she could stop herself.

He laughed and shrugged once again. "Honestly, Lady Brookenham, I do not know."

The sound of him using her title surprised her. It was how he had addressed her when he had kissed her. The memory of his lips on hers filled her with a sudden warmth. That had been such a surprise. But she had not had time to examine it. To discover what she thought about the way that kiss had changed something deep inside of her.

"I wouldn't worry, My Dear," he continued. "You will discover yourself. If you are in doubt, think of your sisters and what they would do."

Isobel nodded. That was good advice, although she would never admit it to them of course. She had spent most of her life pointing out when her sisters were wrong. It had always been one of her favorite pastimes. But in this instance, she believed that Brookenham was correct. Just do what Ann or Lydia would do and all would be fine.

She sighed heavily when he returned to reading a report. A sadness flashed through her as she realized that his attention had been pulled away. Married but hours and he had already forgotten about her.

This was to be her life she realized.

Seeing that the fireplace needed to be stirred, she took the poker and bent over to push at the logs.

What was she supposed to do now? she wondered as she put the iron back in its stand. Glancing back over her shoulder she was surprised to find Brookenham staring at her with a strange, almost hungry look.

Her heart jumped as he held her stare. She was unable to pull away as his gaze held her in place. A predatory look that threatened her very soul. Every muscle screamed to run. She could not tell however whether she should run away or into his arms.

The confusion raging inside of her threatened to erupt into a fire. Her heart jumped again when he started to step around his desk and towards her.

She held her breath as a new excitement began to build inside her.

A sudden knock on the door, pulled them both back to reality.

"Yes," Brookenham barked without taking his eyes off of her.

Wesley stepped into the room then paused, obviously surprised to have interrupted them.

"Excuse me, My Lord," Wesley began. The Earl nodded while he continued to hold her stare.

Wesley cleared his throat then continued, "Cook has asked if you wish a formal dinner or would you prefer something lighter here in the study?"

Isobel's heart fluttered as her husband paused before answering. He continued to stare at her before raising a single eyebrow, asking her which did she desire.

Her cheeks grew warm as she frantically tried to discern the right answer. What were a new bride and husband supposed to do in such a situation?

The corners of his mouth twitched at the beginning of a smile as he turned to the butler and said, "Please inform the staff that they are to take the rest of the day off. Break out a cask of wine from the cellar. No ... make it two casks. With my compliments and gratitude for all of their efforts this day."

Wesley didn't miss a beat as he nodded and said, "Of course, My Lord. It will be much appreciated."

Isobel blanched as she realized that her husband had just told the butler he wished to have privacy when he took his new wife to his bed. Could anything be more embarrassing?

"And inform Her Ladyship's maid that she will not be needed until ... let us say noon tomorrow."

Her heart fell. This was really going to happen and everyone would know it was happening at the time. Swallowing hard, she tried to stop her blush and forced herself not to run away in shame.

"Of course, My Lord, My Lady," Wesley said with a slight bow then backed out of the room.

No sooner had the door clicked shut than she turned on him. "How dare you," she said as an anger began to build inside of her.

He smirked then shrugged his shoulders. "There are no secrets in this house. My Dear. And I assumed you did not wish to be interrupted this evening?"

Once again, her cheeks erupted with heat. Did everything have to revolve around this one thing? This bedding of a new wife. It seemed that everyone found it amusing. A joke to be discussed and bantered about.

Huffing out a heavy breath, she turned to once again poke at the fire. As she pushed at the burning logs she heard him approach from behind her. She held her breath.

Lord Brookenham stopped, his massive presence blocking out half the world.

She froze, unable to move. A thousand thoughts and fears danced through her head. All of them leading to something she could not fathom.

"Here," he said as he gently removed the fire iron from her hand and placed it on its holder. Taking her hand, he turned her so that he could smile down at her. "Come with me."

Three simple words, but it broke some spell. She found herself being led from the room and up the stairs.

Chapter Sixteen

"Now?" Isobel whispered when they were half the way up the stairs. Her body buzzed with a strange new anticipation and constant confusion. It was as if she were being pulled in a dozen different directions. How could they do this? Now of all times. It was still daylight.

He laughed gently and nodded.

"But…"

He leaned down and kissed her softly, "Trust me."

Her heart turned over. Could she trust this man? Really? He had always been, if not an enemy, a nemesis. A sparring partner. Now he was her husband, and soon to be her lover. How could she possibly trust him?

Seeing the doubt in her eyes, he reached down and scooped her up to carry her up the remaining stairs.

Her heart jumped to her throat as she felt him cradle her body in his strong arms.

"Trust me," he said again.

She continued to look into his eyes as he carried her to his room. Could she trust this man? It was a question she had never really thought of. But it was at the core of everything.

He would never hurt her. Not intentionally. Of that she was positive. At least not physically.

But for the first time, she realized her heart might be in danger. Much more than she had ever really anticipated.

Seeing her continued gaze, he smirked once again, then nudged his door open and stepped into his room.

Isobel was surprised to see a rather modern man's bedroom. Striped wallpaper, oak furniture, big windows overlooking the grounds. A large fireplace. A giant bed.

Her heart lurched when she saw the bed and remembered what was to happen.

"My Lord…" she began as she frantically tried to think of some way to delay the inevitable. She wasn't ready. Not emotionally.

"James," he said. "Especially in this room. Especially now."

She swallowed hard and nodded. "James …"

The pause drug out as she became lost in his stare. An awkwardness settled over her. Should she tell him no? That they must wait. Could she tell him no? Suddenly, she was not so sure anymore. It was as if he had gained control of her inner thoughts.

He smiled at her as he slowly lowered her feet to the floor.

Her stomach turned over with fear. The room was too bright. She was not properly prepared.

"My Lord," she began, "James, perhaps we should wait. Perhaps we should grow to know each other before ..."

He continued to smile down at her. "Isobel. You have known me for five years."

"Yes, but ..." This was too soon. Too fast. She was not ready.

He sighed, "Neither of us wanted this. But if you are to have a family. If I am to have an heir. There is only one way."

"Yes, but ..."

"Trust me, this is for the best. We do not need to have this between us. This waiting, this awkwardness. The sooner we put it behind us the better."

Her heart fell. This was nothing more than another obligation to him. A duty he must fulfill. The thought sent a shaft of disappointment through her. She had never imagined herself in such a situation. A cold, heartless exchange. Especially not with this man of all people.

"You must but tell me no," he said as he raised an eyebrow. "I will return to London. You can live here with the staff. Your aunt can move back to this house. We will live separate lives."

The thought bothered her on so many levels. No family of her own. Yet, how could she possibly allow him to do the things he must? How could she possibly surrender her body to this man?

Lifting her chin, she looked deep into his eyes and realized, no, she must go through with it. Women throughout history had surrendered themselves. Now it was her time. It would be embarrassing, possibly painful, and not something she would have chosen for herself. But there was no other choice.

Nodding, she said, "Very well. If we must."

He laughed as he shook his head.

Her insides froze as he stepped towards her while continuing to stare into her eyes.

"Trust me," he said. "Follow my lead and all will be well. I promise."

She swallowed hard. Her mouth went dry and her hands trembled.

He smiled again as he removed the pins from her hair, letting it fall to her shoulders. She shivered with his touch as he ran his fingers through her hair. He smiled the entire time but with a new hungry look in his eyes that made her tremble inside.

What was she supposed to do? Stand there? What?

Her mind whirled with a dozen questions until he pushed her hair to the side as he leaned down to kiss her neck. Every question disappeared as she became lost in the sensation of his lips nibbling at her skin.

Without thought, she closed her eyes and allowed herself to enjoy this feeling of specialness. This sensation of intimacy.

"You are very beautiful," he said as he stepped behind her and began to unlace her dress. Pushing it aside he trailed kisses down her shoulder. "Your skin is a soft as a summer cloud."

Isobel's stomach fluttered as her knees grew weak.

His strong fingers finished with the ties of her dress. She gasped and clutched at it as it began to fall.

He smiled and slowly pulled her hands away so that the dress could crumple at her feet.

A coldness tickled her skin as she stood before him in nothing more than her chamise. A frightening nervousness filled her as he stepped back to examine her. His eyes traveling over her from curve to curve.

The predatory look he gave her made her insides grow warm with anticipation. Suddenly, she began to understand some things as she slowly pushed aside the fear to replace it with a strange new want.

While continuing to stare into her eyes, he removed his coat, then reached back and pulled his shirt over his head.

Isobel gasped at the sight of his broad chest. So large and strong. Like a castle wall. So very male. Suddenly she was once again filled with fear.

He smiled back at her and she realized he could read every thought in her head. The fear, the desire, the mix of curiosity. All of it. Doubtless, he had been with many women. He knew what they thought. What they felt. It was so unfair, this advantage he had over her.

Holding her stare, he reached out and pushed her chamise off her shoulder and then down over her breasts.

She gasped once again, her hands instantly covering herself. This time, he did not push her hands away. Instead, he stepped back and lowered his pantaloons.

Isobel couldn't stop herself from focusing on his manhood. It was so large. It will never fit was her first thought. Followed immediately by an unbearable urge to take it in her hand. The need to caress it shocked her.

"Lower your hands and let me see you, wife," he said softly.

Isobel took a deep breath and forced herself to move her hands so that she stood before him fully exposed. She had never anticipated this. She had always believed this moment would happen in the dark under the covers.

Her insides jittered with excitement. This openness, this sharing was somehow helping her break through her fear. This physical display was building anticipation and an intimacy that surprised her.

Slowly, his eyes traveled down over her breasts, rested for a moment on the curve of her waist, then continued down over her hips to finish on her sex. His appreciative smile filled her with pleasure. He wanted her, there was no doubt. A sense of power washed through her. This powerful man wanted her.

She studied him, her new husband, she reminded herself. She had always known that he had a strong, powerful body. But to see him now, naked. The man reminded her of a Greek statue from the museum. Only alive, here, hers.

"Come," he demanded as he held out a hand.

Swallowing hard, she allowed herself to be led to the bed.

James pulled the blankets back, she scooted to the far side and turned towards him as a surge of excitement filled her. She was about to learn what it meant to be a woman. Finally, she would discover what all the giggles and whispers, and knowing looks between married women was all about.

She remembered that silly smile Ann would have some mornings.

"God woman," he said as he rested a hand on her waist and leaned forward to take her lips with his.

Isobel sighed internally as his lips devoured her. Without thinking her arms wrapped around his wide shoulders so that she could bring him closer. The touch of his skin next to hers sent a bolt of energy through her. Her nipples grew hard as they rubbed against this broad chest.

He moaned as he wrapped his arms around her, trapping her in his embrace. She melted as a feeling of safety and rightness filled her.

As they kissed, his hand traveled up from her waist to cup her breast. She gasped at the new sensation. She felt him smile at her surprise. Pulling back, he looked deep into her eyes. Then leaned down and took her nipple into his mouth.

"James!" she exclaimed as she threw her head back and became lost in the feeling of being at the center of his world.

He continued to suck and nip as his hand traveled down over her stomach to her very core.

As his finger found her, she froze. Then allowed herself to experience this new, wonderful sensation of her very center being caressed.

His finger slid back and forth as she felt herself swell with need. Every motion pushed her higher, filling her with a need that she had never truly known before.

As his mouth continued to suckle at her breast and his finger began to probe her core, she instinctively reached for his manhood. It was so hard, so strong, she realized with surprise. Like velvet covered steel.

He moaned deep in the back of his throat and she smiled to herself. The thought of taming this man sent a thrill through her.

Breaking from her breast, he looked into her eyes, silently asking if she was ready for the next step.

She bit her lip and nodded. She was ready, she realized. In fact, she was more than ready, she was in need and if he did not hurry, she would scream.

"Please," she whispered.

He smiled a knowing smirk that made her angry, but then his finger touched a special spot and she lost all thought of being angry.

As he continued to rub her very core, driving her higher and higher, he positioned himself between her legs.

Isobel held her breath as he took himself in hand and placed himself against her opening.

Holding her gaze, he began to slowly enter her.

Isobel bit the inside of her cheek as she concentrated on not yelling. It would never fit. It was impossible.

"Relax," he whispered as he gently removed himself then slowly pushed in again, just a little.

Closing her eyes, she forced her body to relax, forced herself to accept this invasion. A thousand thoughts flashed through her mind. He was too big. The feeling of him pushing into her. This was necessary. No, it had stopped being necessary and had become desired. She wanted him inside of her.

Pushing back at him, she silently encouraged him to continue.

Grunting under his breath, he pushed himself into her until he reached her barrier. Then leaning down he took her lips with his as he thrust into her.

"God," she gasped.

He froze in place, his eyes searching hers, silently asking if she was alright.

It felt so strange, she realized. To be filled with him, to be joined together like this. Her body wrapped around him. Then he moved inside of her. Just a little at first, then more, and more. Back and forth and she became lost in a new sensation.

Over and over James thrust into her. Filling her with feelings and thoughts she had never known even existed. Higher and higher. Without thought, she wrapped her legs around him, pulling him deeper, demanding more. Her hands raked his back as she forced him to drive into her again and again.

She was lost. There was just the two of them, pushing each other until suddenly, her world exploded into a thousand lights followed by wave after wave of pure pleasure.

"Yes," he yelled as he thrust one last time and exploded inside of her. His warm seed filling her.

"Yes," she replied as another set of waves washed through her. "Yes," she whispered to herself as he collapsed onto her, their hearts pounded together, chest to chest, body to body.   Man   and   wife.

Chapter Seventeen

Brookenham lay next to his wife and fought to regain his breath. That had been unexpected. He had always known the girl was filled with fire, but he would never have believed she could bring that intensity to their bed.

Although an innocent, she learned quickly. She had embraced the situation. Taking and giving. Who would ever have believed it?

Sighing internally, he reached over and pulled her into the crook of his arm, then kissed the top of her head.

"What are you thinking?" she asked with a hesitant tone.

He laughed, "I was regretting giving the staff the evening off. It seems I have worked up quite an appetite."

She pulled back from him to look into his eyes with a strange expression he couldn't begin to fathom. Shaking her head, she laid back down, but he could tell she was upset at him for some reason.

What had he done now? he wondered. Moments before the woman had been lost in the throes of passion, and now she was unhappy about something. There was no pleasing her.

He dismissed it and settled down to soak of the pleasure of holding a beautiful naked woman in his arms. God, she was perfect. That

176

special combination of purity and passion. He could still remember the tight warmth that had surrounded him as he thrust into her. An embracing velvet that had demanded everything from him.

His stomach rumbled.

Isobel once again leaned up and said, "You weren't teasing, you really are hungry."

He laughed. "I never joke about food."

She frowned then said, "Do you want me to get you something. I am sure I could find something in the kitchen."

Brookenham scoffed and pulled her back down to lay next to him.

"There is no need. I won't waste away I assure you. Besides, Cook would have a fit if she found the Lady of the house snooping through her kitchen."

Isobel sighed heavily. "I forget that I am a Countess. I wonder if I will ever become used to it."

He laughed, "You will be an excellent Countess, I assure you."

There was a long pause then Isobel asked, "How can you be sure?"

He laughed again, "Because you are good at almost everything you do."

Again, there was a long pause. "You said almost, what am I not good at?"

He was tempted to mention something about her sharp tongue. Or the way she had of speaking bluntly at times. Even now, she assumed she was good at everything. Most women would have taken his words as a compliment and left it there. But she wanted to prod and poke until she understood everything.

But then he realized, she really was worried. This was a new side to Isobel. A self-conscious woman worried about meeting expectations. He wondered if she was comparing herself to her sisters. Probably. But she really had no need to be concerned.

"Rest assured. You will be fine. The staff adores you. Everyone we know adores you."

"Not your mother."

He pinched her lightly on her waist. "One thing you need to learn is that now is not the time and this is not the place to discuss my mother. Besides, she will not be a bother. I promise."

She snuggled in closer. He sighed, she fit so well next to him. Who would have ever known that a wife could fit so well? Without forethought, his hand began to caress her hip. Her soft skin pulled at him reminding him of their lovemaking which made him wonder if it was too soon to go again.

She was an innocent, he reminded himself. He must be careful and never demanding. Yet his growing hardness announced his need.

As if reading his thoughts, she turned to him and took him in her hand. She looked up into his eyes, silently asking if this was permissible. That innocent expression pulled at his heart. Knowing that he had been her first sent a sense of specialness through him.

He smiled down at her and sighed heavily.

"Careful Isobel or you will begin something I cannot stop."

She smiled at him then said, "Good."

Had any single word ever sounded more perfect? he wondered as his eyes rolled back.

.oOo.

Isobel felt herself grow ready for him. Was it like this for all women? she wondered. This feeling of power and wanton need.

Licking her lips, she laid her head on his chest as she watched her hand go up and down on his thick shaft.

They did not love each other. Instead, it was a purely animal lust, she realized. But, they were married, so surely such a lust was allowed. The man was so male, it pulled at every part of the feminine inside of her. This need to please and take. This overwhelming desire to join with him. To have him inside of her.

Without warning, he grabbed her around the waist and lifted her up and over him. She gasped as she realized what he intended.

179

He positioned her above him then thrust upward into her.

"God," she moaned as he filled her. "I didn't know this was possible."

He smiled up at her and said, "Oh, there is so much for you to learn and I am so going to enjoy teaching you."

She closed her eyes and fell into a rhythm, determined to control every moment. Concentrating on every detail, every sensation. As she sank down on him, she learned that if she wiggled just right, he would moan with pleasure.

Smiling to herself, she slowly drove him mad until he grabbed her once again about the waist to hold her in place while he pushed himself up into her and exploded.

His throbbing release pushed her over the edge into a beautiful wave of pure pleasure. As he continued to grind into her wave after wave washed over her until she collapsed onto his broad chest.

"You woman, are very unique," he whispered as his arms surrounded her in a cocoon of security.

As she lay in his arms, she couldn't stop herself from wondering if he still had a mistress. Suddenly the thought of sharing him with another woman sent a fear and anger straight through her.

If the woman lived in the village, he must dismiss her, she thought. She would never be able to survive meeting her. And the thought of going through life with that fear hanging over her was too much to contemplate.

No. If he must have a mistress then it must be far away.

The thought filled her with a sadness. If this had been a normal marriage, there would be no mistress. She would never have allowed it. But she couldn't make that demand of him. He had never wanted this marriage. It would be too much to ask.

Many marriages in the ton were not completely monogamous. She well knew. Even the wives took lovers.

She had never wanted such a marriage, but she must be realistic. It would be the only way to stop her heart from being hurt. But she could insist on no such woman in the village. That was well within her rights as a wife, wasn't it?

"What is wrong?" he asked as he frowned at her.

A bolt of fear filled her. How had he known what she was thinking? Was she so transparent? How could she ever live with a man who could read her mind?

He laughed at her confusion. "You bite your lip when you worry. You always have. Even as a young girl. What is bothering you?"

181

She shook her head, completely unable to broach the subject. After all, how was a wife supposed to tell her husband that he must dismiss his mistress?

"It is nothing," she said as she slid off of him and onto the bed, making sure her back was to him so that he could not read her thoughts.

He snorted, "Another thing you are going to have to learn. The best time to ask a man for something is just after being intimate with him. We are sort of confused and befuddled and are likely to say yes to anything you ask for."

She felt her heart pound in her chest. How had she allowed this to happen? Moments before they had been so close and now there was this between them.

"It is nothing," she said as she pulled the blankets up to cover herself.

He scoffed then turned over to pull her into a tight embrace.

"Sleep Isobel," he whispered, "you will tell me when you are ready."

Isobel sighed internally as she took his arm and held it just below her breasts. No, she realized. It was a subject she would never broach. Not now.

If he refused, she would be heartbroken. No. it was better to pretend that no such woman existed.

Sighing, she allowed herself to relax in his arms and sink into a deep sleep. The kind of sleep filled with the hopes and fears of a new wife.

Isobel woke the next morning to find the bed cold and empty. She whimpered in frustration. She would have liked to wake with him there. It would have been a special moment. Their first morning together.

But he was gone. A sadness filled her. Her wedding night was over. That one special day had ended. Now the rest of her life was to begin.

What now? she wondered.

Glancing at the shadows in the room it looked to be mid-morning she realized. Of course, the man was up and about. He was probably starving and even now bothering cook for breakfast.

A soft knock from the adjoining room startled her until she realized it was probably Maggie.

"Yes," she called out.

Maggie opened the door and looked in hesitantly. Obviously worried about what she would find. A blithering emotional disaster. Or a dazed woman without her faculties.

Smiling at the maid, Isobel wrapped a blanket around her as she swung her legs over the side of the large bed.

"My Lady," Maggie said with a quick curtsy. "I have a bath ready."

Isobel sighed. Yes, her new life. "Thank you," she said. "I will be there in a moment."

Maggie's brow furrowed in confusion then she nodded as she backed out of the room, closing the door behind her.

Isobel took a moment to gather herself. Was she with child already? she wondered. If so, then they need not repeat the act. The thought disturbed her enough for her to realize how important it had been to her.

Suddenly, a sick feeling filled her as she realized just how much she had enjoyed her new husband and what it would mean if this was to be the last time she shared his bed.

Chapter Eighteen

As Isobel made her way downstairs she debated with herself whether to eat breakfast or find her husband first. Reluctantly, she chose to have a meal first. There was no telling where Brookenham might be.

Wesley met her at the dining room door and smiled.

"Good morning, My Lady," he said with a slight bow.

Isobel smiled back. "Yes, it is," she said to him as she made her way into the room. Her heart fell slightly when she found it empty. No Earl.

"Your customary?" the butler asked. Isobel nodded. For a brief moment, she remembered her childhood. It had been her chore to wake before her sisters and aunt and start the kitchen fire. Now, she sat in a finally decorated mansion with servants waiting on her.

Sometimes, life could be very strange.

"Has His Lordship broken his fast?"

Wesley frowned for a moment before he could hide it.

"Yes, My Lady. Hours ago."

Her stomach tightened up. Why the frown? What did Wesley not wish to tell her?

"And where is he now?" she asked as she took a bite of eggs.

"He left to tour the estate, My Lady. And I believe he intended to stop at the village to take care of some business or other."

Her heart finished falling all the way. The Village? What business could he possibly have there? His mistress? she thought as a bolt of anger shot through her. Had he left their bed to visit his mistress? Surely not.

Yet, what did she know of this man? He was rumored to be voracious in his pursuit of women. Everyone knew his reputation. A fact that never seemed to bother him. Was that what he was doing at the moment? Visiting his mistress.

Who was she? Taking a moment, she checked off a list of possible women. Lauren, the tavern wench. She remembered Ann turning her nose up at the mention of the woman's name when they were younger.

Or perhaps, the widow Carter. She had lost her husband in the war. Yet she was still young and very pretty. Also fair with blue eyes. Brookenham's preferred conquest.

No, she told herself. He wouldn't. Or would he? The doubt and worry tore at her insides. Hadn't she been enough for him? She had given herself to him three times and he had seemed to enjoy it immensely.

No, not a mistress. Not today at least. What then?

Taking another bite of food, she wrestled with herself. Should she confront him? Or ignore it. Theirs was not a true marriage she reminded herself. Did she have any right to make demands of him?

These and a thousand other thoughts rushed through her mind as she continued eating. She had almost finished when the door behind her opened and Brookenham stepped in. Shooting her a quick smile.

Her heart jumped. The man looked so powerful. So commanding. A black frock coat over a white shirt. Buff breaches and Wellington boots. The man looked every inch, a British Lord.

"Good Morning, My Dear," he said as he waved off a footman and began loading a plate for himself with eggs, sausages, and toast.

"I was told you had already eaten," she said as her brow furrowed.

"That was first breakfast," he said with a smile. "I seem to have worked up quite an appetite."

She felt her cheeks blush at the call back to their previous night. Licking her lips, she stared down at her plate, afraid to look at him and find him smirking at her. She would have died of embarrassment.

"What are your plans for the day?" he asked calmly.

Her heart fell. What were her plans? She had none. Aunt Ester had told her to stay away for a few days. She had no chores that needed doing. The staff would have been appalled if she even tried.

"I don't know really," she said with a shrug of her shoulders. "I suppose I should meet with the staff."

The Earl glanced up at Wesley and raised an eyebrow.

The butler nodded and said, "I will schedule meetings, My Lady."

Isobel smiled her thanks then laid her fork across the top of her plate indicating she was through. Almost immediately, a footman stepped forward to remove it.

Suddenly, she realized her life would be made up of such moments. A staff to see to her every whim interspersed with casual conversations with a man who didn't care for her. All of it buried out here in the hinterland, far from London and her friends or family.

She glanced over at her husband as he took a bite of food and felt her heart shift just a little. He had purpose. Seeing to the estates. Serving in Parliament. A reason for being.

"How were your travels, this morning?" she asked only to end the awkward silence.

He shrugged his shoulders. "I visited Tom Waters. He's keeping that prize Hereford bull I purchased. I really do think the beast will go a long way to improving the heard."

She nodded absently as she ran a map of the area through her mind. The local inn was located on the opposite side of the estates from the Water's farm. As was the widow Carter.

"And then," he continued, "I stopped by the blacksmith's in town. I want to change the wooden gates at the bottom of the hill. Replace them with wrought iron. Put the family crest on them. I saw it at the Earl of Devon's last year. Thought it looked ... upscale, shall we say. Besides, the man just had twins, he could use the business."

He is good at this, being an Earl, she realized with a little surprise. She also thought back to when he had arrived at the main house almost six years earlier. A brand new British Lord with no training nor experience. He had come a long way.

Plus, there was his work in Parliament. She remembered Norwich complimenting him on arranging the passage of a bill reforming the prisons and establishing rules of conduct for the King's wardens.

Then she remembered the incident in the alley by the museum. The man had been a heroic beast saving both herself and Maggie.

No, it seemed her husband was a man of many talents. Without warning, her thoughts flashed back to the previous night in his bed and her cheeks grew very warm. Yes, many talents.

"I have a favor to ask," he said as he took another bite.

"Yes?" she answered hesitantly.

He took a deep breath and put his fork down to focus on her.

"I wish to change all of the drapery throughout the house."

Isobel's mind balked for a moment as she reran what she had heard. Had he really asked for her to change all the drapes in the house? Who would have ever believed the Earl Of Brookenham would care for such matters? It seemed too... too ... domestic.

He laughed at the shocked expression on her face.

"There are a great many widows in the village. That damn war, and the sickness that passed through a few years ago..."

She fought to wrap her mind around what he was saying.

"... I thought we could hire them to create new drapes for the house. Julia Carter would be an excellent person to organize them."

Her mind snapped back into focus. Julia Carter? Was he really suggesting she hire his mistress?

"Couldn't we obtain them from London?" she asked as she desperately fought to understand the meaning behind his plan. Then a new thought crossed her mind. No, if the woman was his mistress, she would not need to find ways to earn a living.

The realization that she could cross one woman off the list of possible mistresses made her smile.

"So, you like the idea?" he asked, obviously misreading her happy expression.

"Yes, My Lord. It sounds wonderful."

"Good," he said as he pushed back from the table. "Now, if you will excuse me. There is correspondence waiting for me in my study."

"Of course, My Lord," she said as her mind was already mentally going over what she would need to do. Suddenly, things didn't seem so dire. She had the beginning of a purpose. And if she could make this work. Perhaps there were other things she could do to make life easier for those less fortunate.

Yes, life as a Countess had its benefits she realized.

For the rest of the day, Isobel held meetings with the senior staff. Cook was her normal stern self. Misses Cutler, the housekeeper was much more open to questions and suggestions. But really, the house ran itself. All she need do was remark about her desires and the staff would ensure it happened.

Once, the meetings were done, she and Wesley toured the entire manor from attic to wine cellar. She was determined to learn everything as fast as possible. It was vital that she assume her responsibility and knowledge was the key.

She had barely settled in her parlor after thanking Wesley when Maggie entered the room and frowned at her slightly.

"Yes?" she asked her maid.

"Do you wish to dress for dinner, My Lady?" The young girl asked. Obviously suggesting that she do so or else.

Isobel blanched as she looked out the window and realized how late it had become. What would Lord Brookenham expect? she wondered. When his mother was in residence, she had insisted everyone dress for dinner. Would Brookenham maintain that custom?

"I saw his Lordship's valet preparing his clothes, My Lady," Maggie said.

Isobel's heart softened, her friend knew her so well that she could read her mind with but a look.

"Yes, I will be up shortly," she said. Maggie smiled and dipped into a quick curtsy before leaving.

Never forget, Isobel thought to herself. The staff wants you to succeed. They want Brookenham's estate and household to be something to be proud of. Everyone worked so hard. Not just for the Lord and Lady. All out of a sense of pride.

The thought was humbling. It didn't really matter who the temporary residents were. The staff would still have performed their excellent service. Do not forget that, she told herself. It isn't Isobel Stafford they serve. It is Countess, Lady   of   Brookenham.

Chapter Nineteen

Lord Brookenham allowed his valet to tie his cravat. Really this was ridiculous. His mother was no longer here to demand such stupid practices. But perhaps Isobel expected such things. Heaven knew women did enjoy dressing up for dinner.

It would have been different if they were in London. A house full of guests, or dining before going out for the evening. But here in the country, it had always seemed a little ridiculous dressing just for dinner.

Oh, well. Customs must be maintained, he supposed.

How long would he have to stay here at Brookenham, he wondered. He had promised to remain long enough to get his wife with child. It was the least he could do. After all, Isobel had not wanted this marriage either.

As he examined himself in the mirror one last time he sighed heavily. The thought of his wife troubled him. Their time together last night had been special. Much better than he could have hoped. Most men would consider themselves more than fortunate to have such a wife.

Beautiful, intelligent, kind.

But … The thought of being trapped still remained. That feeling of wondering what he was missing. Even now, many of his friends

194

were carousing and enjoying the nightlife of London while he was stuck here at Brookenham.

Of course, there were some benefits, he thought to himself with a smile.

When he opened the door to the parlor to escort Isobel into dinner, he couldn't help but smile as she looked up at him. Yes, there were some benefits to remaining here a short while longer. The woman looked enchanting.

A sky blue dress, her auburn hair up, exposing a long flawless neck. Pert breasts and shapely hips. Yes, some benefits indeed. His wife was beautiful.

"You are late," Isobel said with a slight shake of her head.

And she had a sharp tongue, he reminded himself.

"My Dear," he began. "I assure you, they will wait for us."

She shook her head. "That is beside the point. Cook and her staff have worked very hard to prepare our meal. The least we could do is respect their efforts."

He sighed heavily. Would it always be like this? he wondered.

"Yes, well, I am here now," he said as he held out an arm to escort her to the dining room.

Rising gracefully, she placed her hand on his arm and let him lead her out of the parlor.

"It is just that I believe it is important that we not take advantage of the staff," she said, continuing to press her point.

He sighed heavily and drew to a stop. Turning to her, he frowned down at her and shook his head. "Isobel," he said. "I have agreed with you. There is no need to belabor the issue."

She blanched for a second, obviously upset at being corrected.

Seeing that she understood him, he turned and led her to the dining room. As they were being seated he couldn't help but notice her shoot him a quick glance from beneath her brow. She was obviously unsure of herself.

The look she gave surprised him. She was nervous, he realized. Why? They had made it through the wedding night without incident. Rather enjoyably, he thought. They had passed the day without a major disagreement. Surely it wasn't the small discussion in the hall. No, something else was bothering her.

"So, after dinner. Would you like to join me in a game of Whist," he asked. "Or we could always retire early," he added with a smirk.

Her cheeks grew beet red as she glanced at the footman and Wesley.

His new wife was easily embarrassed, he realized. A fact that he must keep in his pocket and pull out when needed.

"A game of Whist sounds nice," she said before taking a spoonful of soup. "Or perhaps a game of chess?"

Now it was his turn to balk.

"Did Norwich teach you?" he asked hesitantly.

"Yes," she answered as she gave him a quick smile. But there was a knowing look behind her eyes. If he was not mistaken, this woman would be a difficult opponent. If Norwich had taught her, then she would be very difficult.

"Very well," he said. "A game of chess does sound nice."

She smiled back at him, the awkward moment in the hall forgotten.

As he studied her for a quick second, he suddenly realized that he was disappointed she hadn't chosen to retire early.

Once they were finished with their meal, he escorted her to the parlor. He threw a log onto the dwindling fire while Isobel arranged the pieces on the chess board. He despised waiting for the staff to maintain the fire. He was perfectly capable.

"You know, Lady Brookenham," he said as he sat down across from her, "normally, I have found that games are much more enjoyable if there are stakes attached." Raising an eyebrow, he silently informed her of what he was thinking.

Her cheeks grew pink as she focused on the board in front of her.

"Such as?" she asked finally as she moved her rook's pawn.

"Oh, I don't know," he said as he countered her move. "What do you have to wager?"

She laughed and shook her head. "You know very well that the moment I said my vows you took ownership of all I possess. Even my pin money is an allowance from you."

Her words made him pause. She was correct. Legally everything she owned was his to do with as he wished. It must trouble her, he thought. How could it not?

"It need not be monetary in nature," he said as he continued to look at the board, then moved his bishop out on the attack.

A long silence hung in the air.

"What then?" she asked as she made her move. Then, looked up and raised her own eyebrow. Silently pushing things higher.

His heart jumped. The woman was a bit of a temptress. Who would have ever known?

"Well," he began. "I suppose there are always … services we could provide each other. Something special. Something … beyond the normal, shall we say."

Her face grew white as she stared at him. Obviously, things had gone farther, faster than she had anticipated.

"Such as?" she asked hesitantly.

He shrugged his shoulders. "That would be up to you."

Isobel continued to look back at him with a pale face and big eyes. "I wouldn't know what to ask for," she said as a faint blush rushed to her cheeks.

He laughed. "Oh, give me time, My Dear. Give me time."

The blush grew even deeper as she looked down at the board, afraid to meet his gaze.

"I know," she said with a sudden burst of happiness. He froze, surprised at her reaction.

"What would you request?" he asked, immensely curious.

She took a deep breath. "You will attend church with me on Sunday. You never go. The people of the village have noticed. I can assure you."

He scoffed. "You know I don't attend church. It is one of the benefits of being an Earl. I can ignore those things I don't care for."

"Regardless," she said. "If I win, you must attend church with me on Sunday."

Brookenham took a deep breath and nodded. Then he smiled to himself. Isobel caught that smile and froze, her hand above a pawn.

"What will you demand?" she asked. "If you win."

What should he ask for? he wondered. The woman was already his wife. He could demand anything within expected bounds. It did take some of the joy out of the chase.

He slowly smiled at her. "That you allow me to make love to you, here in the parlor."

Her face drained of all color. "Here? Not in your room? Do things such as that happen?"

The Earl laughed and shook his head. "I assure you, they do."

"But we may be discovered," she said with disbelief.

"That adds to the excitement," he replied, continuing to smile at her.

She stared down at the board then said, "Very well," without looking up.

Chuckling to himself, he moved his piece as a new sense of seriousness filled him. It was vital that he win this match. Not only for his own pride, but to show her what was truly possible.

Of course, once the wager had been agreed to, a heavy silence fell over the room as they both fought to win.

She was very good, he realized and would not be easily defeated. The idea of loosing to his new wife was particularly disturbing. Nothing could be allowed that made her think less of him. The thought sent a surprising chill down his spine.

No, he needed an edge, he realized as a plan began to form.

Her hand rested next to the board and her captured pieces. Smiling internally, he reached over and gently rested his hand on hers while he moved his queen. Her fingers were so small and dainty he thought with an internal smile. A woman's hand.

It took her a moment to realize what he had done, but she did not pull away. Instead, she continued to look at the board. But he could tell she had been impacted. The increase in breath. The quick lick of her lips told the story.

Yes, it was beginning to work. Deciding to take it to the next level, he gently began to caress the back of her hand. Simple circles, back and forth. All the while, never looking at her. Never making it obvious.

She hesitated over her move several times. He had to fight not to smile to himself.

At last, she made a quick move using her free hand. Yes, he had her, he realized. She was enjoying his caress and didn't want it to stop.

She was different than most women, he realized. She never fished for a compliment. Never batted her eyelids with false interest. No, Isobel was an open book. A deep, complex book, but open to full discovery.

There was no hidden agenda, he realized. If she thought something, she was unafraid to express herself. As he had well learned over the years. Yet, it was never with a sense of meanness, or spite.

She simply saw the world as the way it should be and was not worried about sharing her opinion. Yes, rather unusual.

"Your skin is as smooth as a summer wind," he said as he smiled at her.

She swallowed hard, but still did not pull away.

Shifting in his chair, he brought his foot to lay next to hers under the table.

He watched as her brow furrowed with concern. But still, she did not pull away. Yes, he thought. Who knew chess could ever be so entertaining?

"And that dress," he said. "Most becoming. But then, a woman as beautiful as you would make any dress particularly fetching."

Her cheeks grew redder but she continued to stare down at the board. Obviously afraid to acknowledge his compliments but basking in them none the less.

Almost there, he thought. She had not seen the trap he had laid for her on the board.

Finally, she made the move he had hoped for. Picking up his rook, he moved it into place and said, "checkmate."

She pulled back, surprised, as she examined the board for an escape. Then looking up at him, her forehead creased into a deep frown.

"You bastard, you seduced me," she said.

He laughed out loud as he placed a hand over his heart. "Who me?" he said with an air of false innocence.

She stared at him with an almost angry look. As if she couldn't believe he would stoop to such a level. Apparently, she didn't know him as well as he had thought.

"What now?" she asked as she finally met his eyes with her own. He could see a hesitant hope hidden behind those eyes.

He smiled. "Now you pay your gambling debts."

Chapter Twenty

Standing, he held out his hand. A warm sense of pleasure passed through him. She was so innocent. So unsure of herself. Yet, beneath it all was a sense of curiosity. Yes, he was going to enjoy this.

Even more important. So was she.

Smiling, he led her to the settee and indicated she should have a seat. She frowned for a moment then sat down primly, arranging her dress about her as she looked up at him with a furrowed brow in confusion.

Glancing over at the door, she swallowed and held her breath.

He laughed.

"Relax, Isobel," he said as he sat down next to her. "I promise, we will not be disturbed." Seeing her shoulders slump slightly in relief, he had to add, "At least I hope not."

Once again, her face grew pale as she swallowed hard. She really was nervous, he realized. The thought of being discovered by the servants in the throes of passion bothered her significantly. He was tempted to relent and take her up to his room. But a need to push her boundaries filled him.

As he sat there next to her, he stopped for a moment and looked deep into her eyes. Holding her stare.

"You are very beautiful, you know," he said. "A man could become lost in your eyes for half his life."

She blushed fiercely and looked down at her hands in her lap.

"But it is your lips I find most enticing," he said as he leaned forward and took her lips with his.

Isobel placed her hands on his shoulders, holding him in place. He smiled internally as a fire began to build inside of him. The woman was intoxicating.

As his hand moved from her waist to gently caress her breast, she moaned in the back of her throat. A deep sound of want and need.

As he kissed and caressed, his hand slid down to the hem of her dress and slowly began to lift it.

For the briefest of moments, she froze as she realized what she was doing. But she did not push him away. Instead, she became lost in his kiss as she pulled him closer.

Brookenham smiled to himself as he gathered the cloth of her dress. Once he had it above her knees, his hand slid along her soft thigh to find her core.

"James," she sighed as his finger gently rubbed her through her small clothes.

Slowly, he built a passion in her. Touching, caressing, nipping at her until he could feel the heat burning inside of her.

Yes, he thought, driving Isobel mad with passion was one of his new favorite things in life. Now, to raise it even higher.

He slid onto his knees before her as he ran kisses down her neck. Her hands clasped his head as her eyes rolled back. The Earl smiled to himself as he pulled back and lowered his lips to kiss the inside of her knee.

Glancing up, he caught her with a confused look. Looking up into her eyes, he held her stare as he slowly removed her undergarments. Her eyes grew wide as she realized just how exposed she was to him.

"Trust me," he whispered as he began to gently push her legs apart so that he might kiss the inside of her silky, smooth thighs.

"James?" she gasped.

He smiled to himself as he brought his lips to her very core. Honey mixed with nectar, he thought as he became lost in her.

"JAMES," she exclaimed as his tongue found her magic button and began to suckle and caress.

Isobel moaned loudly as she began to squirm, searching, enjoying. He could tell the woman was fully engulfed in pure pleasure.

His heart raced as he realized just how much he enjoyed this. The pleasure he was bringing her. The woman was spectacular, she was allowing him to take her to heights she had never expected.

Suddenly, her body went stiff as her hands grabbed his head and held it in place.

"Yes, Yes," she yelled as her entire body began to shake with wave after wave of pleasure. "Oh, yes," she said more softly as she slowly returned to sanity.

A sense of wellness washed over him as he watched her face. The mixture of surprise and wanton need made him chuckle to himself. A man could get used to this he thought. Making his wife lose her senses.

Their eyes met. Isobel stared down at him with a hungry look.

"Please," she said as she pulled him up so that she could wrestle with his pantaloons. "Please," she said again as she took him out and fondled him. Then, once she knew he was ready, she pulled him to her opening, shifting on the settee so that she could take him.

God, the woman was perfect, he thought as he held her in place and pushed himself into her.

Isobel bit her lip and threw her head back. He could tell she was fighting to hold back a scream of pleasure. Instead, she wrapped her legs around him and pulled his head down so she could take his lips with her.

Brookenham became lost himself as he thrust into her over and over, becoming lost in the sleek wetness between her legs. That warm tightness that drove him mad with lust.

"God, Yes," he said as he thrust one last time and exploded. Over and over he filled her with every bit of his soul.

Isobel bit his shoulder as she too began to climax.

The two of them held each other tightly as they allowed the world to dissolve and then once again to come back together.

At last, when his breathing returned to normal, he slowly withdrew only to hear Isobel whine deep in her throat at the thought of losing him inside of her.

"The night is young," he whispered as he kissed her forehead.

She sighed heavily, "Do you think anyone heard us?" she asked with obvious trepidation.

He laughed, "Us? No. You? Probably."

All color drained from her face as her eyes grew as large as dinner plates.

"I am teasing," he said as he realized that if she became upset it might never happen again. "The staff are at their dinner. No one heard anything."

She looked doubtfully into his eyes then relaxed just a little, obviously deciding to believe him. What she didn't know was that he didn't care what his servants heard. She was his wife and he would take her when and where ever he wanted.

Isobel studied him for a moment, her eyes cataloging. Without thinking, she naturally began to bite at her lip. He knew that look well. She was trying to solve a puzzle. Probably wondering what she could criticize next.

As she studied him, he purposely looked down at her exposed body, openly admiring the auburn triangle at the junction of her well-formed thighs.

Isobel gasped as she horridly scrambled to get her dress back in place.

He laughed as he stood and held out a hand to help her up. "No need for modesty, My Dear. Just remember. Every day, when we sit across from each other at the dining table. I will be remembering the way it feels to be inside of you."

She gasped as once again the color drained from her face.

He laughed again as he tucked her hand into his arm and led her upstairs. Yes, he thought, a most remarkable woman.

.o0o.

Isobel woke once again to find her husband missing. It had been this way for three weeks. Every morning she would wake to find him gone. Why couldn't he wait for her?

She had so hoped to snuggle in his arms. But it was as if the sun coming up changed his perspective on their marriage. During the day he would be formal. Or more likely, gone off on estate business. They would have a rather silent dinner, perhaps play cards, then retire for an evening of bliss.

Each cold day followed a hot night. It felt wrong. There was little sharing of secrets or common purpose. None of the special togetherness she had witnessed between her sisters and their husbands.

At times, she felt as if she were nothing more than an object. Something to satisfy his needs.

Yet, it was for her, she reminded herself. It was her desire to have a family that dictated their unions each night. If not for that, he might very well have returned to London long ago, she realized with a sudden sadness.

No, she had no right to complain, she reminded herself. But that did not stop the small sorrow that sat at the bottom of her stomach. It was only half a life. And so not what she had dreamed of.

A thought of Lord Darlington danced into her mind and she shuddered. Things could be so much worse, she told herself. At least with Brookenham, she could always rely upon his honor.

And his wide shoulders that seemed to carry the weight of the world, she added to herself with a smile. She would never forget what he had taken on simply to protect her.

Sighing, she glanced at the window and realized she had slept late again. Where had all of her energy gone? She had always been one of the first up and about. But, of late, it seemed like it took a great deal of effort to get out of bed each morning.

Of course, the attention of her husband each night might have had something to do with her lack of energy during the day.

As she slipped on her robe, she called out for Maggie. If she hurried she would have time to visit Aunt Ester. She made a point of seeing the older woman at least twice a week. Her aunt still refused to move up to the main house and Isobel had given up trying to convince her. So, she would spend the afternoon twice a week sitting with her aunt, discussing nothing important. Simply sharing time together.

"Are you feeling well, My Lady?" Maggie asked with a strange expression as she stepped into the room with a simple gray dress draped over her arm.

"Yes, of course," Isobel answered as she began to wash.

Maggie continued to study her for a long moment then seemed to accept the fact that her employer was perfectly well.

Isobel could only shrug as she hurried to get downstairs, suddenly she had a strong urge for the cook's special sausage. The thought of the spicy concoction made her mouth water.

As she had feared, Brookenham was not there when she entered the dining room.

"Just sausage and toast," she told Wesley, "no eggs this morning."

She sighed internally. She had learned not to ask. It was always the same, Wesley wincing and then telling her His Lordship had left much earlier.

He probably thought it strange that a wife did not know what her husband was up to. But at least he wasn't spending his time with a mistress she thought with a small smile. The man wouldn't have the energy.

In addition, she had met with the Widow Carter about the drape project and discovered the woman to be perfectly sweet. Isobel considered herself a strong judge of character, and it was impossible to believe a woman could look her squarely in the eye if she was sleeping with her husband.

No, he wasn't spending time with a mistress. Not unless she was to consider the Estate itself a mistress. All of his time and effort were wrapped up in improving things. Both for the estate and for the tenants.

Once again, she sighed heavily as she began on the cook's sausage. Only after she had finished a second helping did she say to the butler, "I will be visiting my aunt this afternoon. Unless you know of something I have forgotten?"

"No, My Lady," Wesley said as he pulled back her chair. "You have that meeting with the church council tomorrow."

She winced, she had still not been able to convince His Lordship to attend the local church. It was embarrassing to arrive each Sunday alone, she thought to herself as a sick apprehension filled her.

 She knew perfectly well that the ladies would tiptoe around the subject. But the luncheon could not be avoided. Not if she was to have the influence in the village she wanted.

Smiling her thanks to Wesley and John the footman, she gathered a shawl from the parlor and started for her aunt's cottage. It was a beautiful day. A high blue sky with just enough of a breeze to keep things cool.

A faint hint of summer wafted through the air. A combination of dry dust, freshly plowed fields in the distance, and new roses.

As she walked through the apple orchard, she couldn't help but smile. This place had been so important to her family. It was where Ann had met Norwich. That chance meeting had changed everything. Allowing Lydia to meet the Duke of Cambridge, and if she was honest with herself, it had ultimately led to her own marriage with Brookenham.

Yes, a special place.

Once through the orchard, she began to hurry down the path until she came into sight of her old home. A small country cottage with a thatched roof and a picket fence. The roses were in full bloom and a faint hint of smoke rose from the chimney.

The savory scent of freshly baked bread made her stomach growl.

Misses Peele, her aunt's helper, must be baking she realized as she walked through the gate.

"Aunt Ester," she called out as she stepped inside. This was her home, the thought of knocking first seemed wrong somehow.

"Isobel," her aunt answered as she stepped around the corner.

Isobel relaxed slightly. It appeared her aunt was having one of her better days. There was no sign of the confusion that afflicted her at times.

Bending slightly, Isobel gave her aunt a long hug then smiled down at her.

Aunt Ester's eyes narrowed for a long moment, then she reached up and laid a hand on Isobel's neck and said, "You are with child."

Isobel's world came to a skidding halt as she said, "No. I can't be. Not this fast."

Aunt Ester laughed and shook her head. "I can tell. I always know. When were your last courses?"

Isobel swallowed hard as she frantically counted off the days and realized she was a week past due.

Had that been why Maggie had stared at her strangely this morning? Had her maid realized she was late? Might she have been curious to know if her mistress had morning sickness?

No. It was impossible. But the signs were there she realized. Her lack of energy. The strange food cravings, her missed monthly event. Even her breasts felt tender.

Could it be true? Was she really with child? The thought sent a burst of pure happiness through her. This had been what she had wanted. What she had prayed for

And now it was hers.

Suddenly, a cold realization washed over her. What would James do when she told him? There would no longer be a need for him to stay at Brookenham. He could return to London and resume his life.

She would no longer share an evening meal with him. There would be no more card games or quiet evenings in the garden over the chess board. She would no longer be able to watch him play with Sam, the barn dog. Or, secretly observe him when he dismissed the stable boys and curried his horse himself.

When asked why, he had simply shrugged his shoulders and said he did his best thinking pulling a brush over a horse's back.

She had no sooner pictured him in the barn that she flashed to their nights together. The thought sent a cold chill down her spine as she realized she would no longer be sharing his bed every night.

A cold dread filled her at the realization she had fallen in love with her husband and he was going   to   leave   her.

Chapter Twenty-One

Isobel stopped when she reached the apple orchard. Her feet refused to move forward.

How could she have been so foolish. Falling in love had never seemed possible, Yet, here she was. A woman completely in love with a husband who did not share the same feelings.

Such a fool.

Should she tell him about the child? Over and over her mind worked at the issue. No, not yet. She might be mistaken. No need to start actions in motion. Not yet.

But! If she didn't, would that not be a form of deceit? He took her to his bed to get her with child. If she was with child already, then he had no need to perform such an act.

What were the rules in such a situation? she wondered.

Shaking her head, she turned to continue pacing. Her slippers and the hem of her dress grew damp from the wet grass, but she couldn't stop as her stomach turned over.

No, she couldn't lay with him. Not now. It would not be right. Not unless she told him the truth.

But if she did, he would leave and she would be without him anyway. At least this way she could keep him here in Brookenham a little bit longer.

Again, the decision to remain quiet seemed false and unfair.

The awareness of the strong feelings flowing through her made everything tingle. She was in love with a man who felt nothing but duty towards her. A man whose life was centered elsewhere. Not her and not her child.

Shouldn't she let him know the truth so that he could return to his life? Hadn't she asked enough of him already?

The thought made her sigh heavily.

How could she look him in the eye if she knew she was keeping this truth from him?

But the thought of him leaving for London tore at her heart. And knowing that he would soon be sharing some other woman's bed filled her with an anger and frustration that threatened to explode.

Once again, she turned and slapped at an apple hanging just above her head. The fruit flew across the orchard to land with a thump and roll next to another tree. Isobel ignored it, her mind was wrestling with itself and loosing.

And there was no one to talk to about it. The pregnancy, the child inside of her, whether she should tell her husband or not.

No one. Ann and Lydia were too far away. Aunt Ester would never really understand. She was a spinster who had never been in love. Especially not with a man who did not love her back.

218

Aunt Ester would have no concept of the hurt and hope tumbling over each other deep inside of her. No thought on what it meant to love a man and lose him. No, her aunt would be of no benefit.

Isobel sighed heavily then set her shoulders and started for the main house. No, she wouldn't tell him. Not yet. But, she would no longer share his bed either. It was the only honorable way through this glorious, yet prickly, situation.

Later that night as they sat alone on the veranda with a chessboard between them, she studied her husband and realized he had the potential to be a good father. Kind, yet firm. A tower of strength who could enjoy life.

A sense of fear began to eat at her insides though. A family had been her desire, not his. He had never wished children. What if he became cold and distant to the child? What if he simply did not care.

The thought sent a bolt of pure protectiveness through her. No, her baby would be cherished by their father. She refused to accept any other result.

As she watched, his forehead creased in concentration while he studied the board. She had positioned her pieces well and he was having difficulty devising a plan to extract himself.

Her stomach turned over as she thought about what she must say. There really was no way to approach the subject tenderly other than to simply come out and say it.

"I will not be sharing your bed tonight," she said as she watched him intently.

He pulled back, his eyes narrowed in confusion and what she hoped was a slight disappointment. He continued to look at her for a long moment then nodded his acceptance.

"Of course," he said. "I understand."

She sighed internally. He probably believes I am starting my time of the month, she realized. What would he think if he learned the truth?

He smiled slightly to her then returned to focusing on the board before him.

Really? That was how he reacted? she thought with surprise. No trying to argue her out of it. No questions about how long she might be absent from his bed. Not one word about missing their time together. No, nothing more than he understood.

The man could be as dense as a brick at times, she thought as she ground her teeth.

As the game progressed, she fought with herself to stop from telling him about the baby. Perhaps that could elicit a reaction. But no, he might not react as she hoped. It was best she wait, she finally realized. At least a few days.

Her mind drifted as she thought about the child growing inside of her. Was it a boy or a girl? she wondered. What would they be like? Would they look like James? These and a thousand other questions danced through her head.

Later, as she looked up, she caught her husband giving her a strange look.

"What?" she asked.

"What happened?" he said, nodding at the board between them.. "You had me trapped, then it was as if you stopped caring and let me get out of it? Why? It is not like you. Normally you are a relentless terror."

Her heart stopped, she had forgotten about the game, becoming lost in her own thoughts.

Shrugging her shoulders, she shook her head. "My mind is elsewhere tonight. It happens."

Lord Brookenham studied her for a long moment then said, "I suppose every new husband must discover new things about his wife the first month of their marriage."

"Yes, well," she said as she rose from her chair, "never believe you have discovered everything. No man is that intelligent."

He laughed.

He laughs well, she thought. With ease and honesty. Sighing internally, she realized she needed to escape before she changed her mind and joined him in his bed.

"Goodnight," she said with a small smile then turned and left, but as she stepped back into the house, she silently prayed he would call her back. Prayed that he would refuse to be without her. But of course, there were no such words. No declaration.

A sadness filled her as she realized the rest of her life would be like this. Secretly wanting more. Desperate for any sign of attention.

Isobel was able to make it all the way to her own room before a tear began to form in the corner of her eye. She loved the man and the thought filled her with sadness.

That night, she lay awake in her own bed, punching her pillow as she desperately searched for a comfortable position that would allow her to sleep. James was in the next room. Only feet away, but she could not go to him.

An animalistic urge burned inside of her. A need to be taken by him. But she pushed the feeling away. Instead focusing on the child growing inside of her.

The next morning, she was still awake, staring into space, when Maggie stepped into the room and gasped to find her mistress sleeping in her own bed.

"Is everything alright, My Lady?" Maggie hissed as she glanced to the side door that entered the master suite. The look of protective caring that flashed across the maids face filled Isobel with a sense of warmth. The young girl would fight hell itself if it meant protecting her mistress.

"Yes, everything is well," Isobel said with her best reassuring voice.

Maggie halted for a second as her eyes narrowed while she studied Isobel, obviously not completely believing her.

"Is it the child?" the maid asked.

Isobel gasped. "You know?"

Maggie nodded as she bit her lip, waiting for an answer.

"Partly," Isobel replied. "I have not told His Lordship," she hurriedly added. "You mustn't say a word."

The maid continued to frown but finally said, "Of course, My Lady. But, he is going to learn eventually. I mean ..."

Isobel laughed to herself at the thought of trying to hide a pregnancy.

"Of course, he will learn. The entire world will get to see me as large as one of His Lordship's Prize Herefords. But not yet. You must promise."

"I promise," the maid said as she opened the armoire to retrieve a dress for the day.

Isobel sighed internally. It felt good to tell someone. Perhaps she should write to Ann and Lydia. Surely, they could offer advice.

The thought made her smile to herself. She had always hated when her sisters gave her advice. Simply because they were older and had experienced things before her was no reason they should be allowed to pretend they knew things she didn't.

But in this case. Perhaps it was best to seek their counsel. Heaven knew she was clueless when it came to being pregnant.

Of course, who she should really tell was her husband, she realized. In truth, that was why she had tossed and turned through the night. Keeping secrets from him tore at her insides. A guilty conscious had always been her downfall.

Ann used to say that she needn't worry about who committed mishaps about the house. Isobel would tell on herself. Lydia would hide it. Ann simply had to wait. She would know within the hour. Either Isobel would confess. No confession, then obviously, Lydia had committed the offense.

Lydia hated the fact that she couldn't get away with anything by throwing doubt on the situation.

Sighing, she silently determined that she must tell James the truth. Granted, he might leave her. But she could no longer hide this from him.

Of course, the man was nowhere to be found. He had departed earlier that morning and informed Wesley he would not return until late.

Why couldn't he have told her that? she wondered as she paced back and forth in the parlor. Did he care so little that he couldn't even take a moment to keep his own wife informed of his whereabouts and plan?

The thought ate at her soul as she continued to pace.

Oh, how things had changed. How she had changed. A month earlier she was a young woman searching for a husband. But her own woman in a sense. Able to make decisions for herself. At least as much as society and the Duke of Norwich would allow.

Now, she was a married woman with a child on the way. A woman with a husband who didn't love her and would quickly leave for the wonderful life of London.

She had wanted a family, and it appeared she would have one. Yet, deep inside, it didn't match up to all she had hoped. There was a sense of unity missing. Instead, it would be her alone facing the world. For all practical purposes, she would be raising the child by herself. Of course, with a dozen servants to help.

But it would be her decisions. Where as before, she had never worried about making the right one. Now, she felt a sense of terror at the thought of doing this alone.

Sighing to herself she retrieved a book from the library and forced herself to wait patiently. After dinner, she thought. She would tell him after dinner.

Of course, throughout dinner, she had to constantly bite her tongue every time she caught his eye. This was news that could not be shared in front of the staff.

He looked differently tonight she realized. More serious, more concerned. He was quieter than normal. Focused on his food. Occasional glancing up, catching her eye, frowning, then returning to his meal.

What was it? she wondered. Surely, he wasn't upset about their night apart. No, something else was bothering him. Sighing internally, she congratulated herself on being able to read her husband. She was learning his moods.

"Chess?" he asked as he pushed back from the table after finishing his meal.

Isobel nodded, suddenly unable to speak as a fear bubbled up inside of her. This was to be a turning moment she realized.

He thanked Wesley, then escorted her to the garden terrace. It had become their favorite location to spend the evening. A place of privacy. Surrounded by rose bushes and the distant call of birds from the orchard down below.

"James," she began as she started to arrange the pieces.

"Yes," he answered without looking at her.

Her heart stopped as she took a deep breath. "I need to tell you something."

His hand froze above his rook as he slowly looked at her.

It must be now, she thought to herself or she would never get it out. There were a dozen different reactions he could have and almost all were bad but it could not be avoided. Not if she was to live with herself.

Staring into his eyes she said, "Um ... I believe I am with child."

He winced as if she had slapped him. But then recovered quickly and smiled slowly. "Are you sure?"

She let out a long sad breath. That wince of his had hurt. But it was the smile that killed her. It was a smile of relief. He had accomplished his goals and he no longer needed to bed her every night. It could mean nothing else.

"Yes, I am sure," she said. "Or at least I believe so," she added as she looked down at her pieces and fought to hold off a tear. This should be a special moment between them. A time they could recall in the future with fondness and a shared sense of togetherness.

Instead, it seemed to be nothing more than a casual conversation.

"So, I am to suppose that this is why you slept in your own bed last night," he asked.

She nodded as a sad sick feeling filled her. "Sharing a bed is no longer necessary," she managed to say.

From across the table, she heard him sigh heavily. Her heart hardened as she awaited his reply.

"Actually," he began as she held her breath. "This makes my decision easier."

Her brow furrowed in confusion.

"I must return to London. Even Norwich and Cambridge are going back. Things are getting out of hand. Several of us are hoping to convince Liverpool that reforms are the only thing that can stop us from copying the French and slipping into a terrible revolution.

London. He was going back.

"Is it really that bad?" she asked, desperately hoping that he would change his mind.

He sighed and nodded sadly. "I am sorry, but it is. Between the famine in Ireland two years ago, the clearances in the Scottish Highlands. The men returning from the war with no work and the widows and orphans begging in the streets. Yes, things were getting worse. People are starting to organize. If we don't do something, there is no telling where the country will end up."

She frowned to herself as she wrestled with what he had said, suddenly her fears and silly worries didn't seem that important.

"Liverpool and most of the other Lords believe things can be kept under control by the use of force. Several of us, Norwich, Cambridge and I believe otherwise. We must reform now before we are forced to do so after a violent upheaval."

Her world was crashing around her. He was leaving her to return to his old life. Suddenly her stomach threatened to rebel. She couldn't take this. Not now.

Pushing her chair back while holding a hand to her mouth. She mumbled an apology as she rushed from the room.

He didn't come after her. He didn't seem to care enough.

This was to be her life she realized.

Alone.

Chapter Twenty-Two

Lord Brookenham paced his study and cursed under his breath. He needed to be off, but Isobel had still not come down.

It seemed rude to leave without saying goodbye. Especially after the woman had informed him that she was carrying his child.

Once again, she had slept in her own bed. The thought angered him at a deep level. But it was her words that hurt him to the very quick. 'It is no longer necessary.'

That was all he was to her. A means to an end. A child of her own. It was all she had wanted and he had given it to her so now he was no longer necessary.

His hands clenched up into fists. That was all he would ever be to her. A man to save her honor, give her a child, pay the bills and nothing more.

Thankfully, London would salve his wounded pride. He would make sure of it.

He turned to retrace his steps when he heard a door close upstairs. Finally, he thought as he threw open the door and looked up the stairs to see his wife slowly descending. His heart hitched for the slightest second. The woman was beautiful. And she was carrying his child, he reminded himself.

A possessive, protectiveness washed over him. The mother of this child. His insides turned over as he realized just how important she had become to him.

Yet, he had been dismissed. Him, an Earl. Set aside, no longer needed. To use her own words — no longer necessary. Those words would rumble around in the back of his brain for a long time to come, he realized.

She smiled hesitantly down at him. He held his breath, there were a thousand things to say. But none of them seemed appropriate for the moment. Instead, he waited until she joined him.

"You are leaving?" she said with a hint of surprise.

"Yes, if I hurry I can be there before dark."

She bit her lip and stared up at him for a long moment then nodded. She seemed worried, he thought. Why? She had what she wanted, or at least soon would.

"Let me guess," she said. "You have the horse saddled and have been waiting for me. You should have told me, I would have come down earlier."

He shrugged. Somehow, her tardiness had become his fault. It was of no mind, he thought to himself. Soon he would be away and they could both return to their own lives.

"I am but a day away if you need me," he said. "Send John, he is the fastest rider."

"I am sure I will be fine."

His heart jumped a beat as he realized she would be just fine without him. This was Isobel, he reminded himself. The most independent woman he knew. She would be fine without him. In fact, she would thrive.

"Yes, well, I will be off then."

The two of them paused as they looked into each other's eyes. Finally, she pulled her gaze away and said, "Please tell your mother of our news. I know it will please her."

He froze for a second until he realized she was talking about the child. Yes, his mother would be pleased.

"Of course," he told her. "But you do realize the news will ignite another wave of rumors. Everyone will assume that the child will come early. Very early."

She smiled sadly and shrugged her shoulders. "In all honesty, I no longer care what people think. Not as long as it does not hurt the child."

He sighed heavily. "It won't, I assure you. I will make sure of it."

Isobel smiled sweetly then reached up to kiss him on the cheek.

That was it, their goodbye. The perfect opportunity to make his break. Yet, still he hesitated. It seemed wrong to leave her like this. As if he were making a fatal error.

But really, he had no other choice. He had given her what she wished. His name, his child, a house filled with servants. No, she had everything she would ever need. He had fulfilled his husbandly duties.

"Take care, Isobel," he said as he patted her on the shoulder and turned to leave. At the door, he turned and gave her one last quick smile, then stepped out into the drive and took the horse from the stableman.

Yet, with each step, each action, he felt himself being torn in two. As he swung his leg up over the saddle, he glanced back at the front door but she hadn't come to wave goodbye. No, they didn't have that kind of connection, he thought with a touch of sadness.

They weren't close enough to miss each other, he thought to himself, but deep down he knew that was a lie. At least on his part.

No. She had her life and he had his.

Sighing, his shoulders slumped in defeat as he started the horse on the road to London. It was going to be a long day.

She had never asked when or even if he would return. No mention of the baby. Nothing. It was as if she had cut him out of her life once he had given her what she wanted. The realization hurt at a gut-churning level.

No, this had not been what he had expected.

It was for the best he told himself. He could return to the life he knew. Now that she had what she wanted, he was free to follow his own choices.

.o0o.

Isobel wiped at the tear in the corner of her eye as she stood at the parlor window to watch him ride away.

He was really leaving. There had been no discussion of when he would return. And obviously, she could not follow him to London. Not in her condition. No, it was as if he couldn't wait to get away. Get back to the life he loved.

A sharp pain gnawed at her heart. It was as if she was of no matter. He had fulfilled his obligations and now she could be dismissed.

The man hadn't even mentioned his own child. They hadn't discussed names. Creating a nursery. None of the shared intimate details about bringing a new life into this world.

As the pain continued to pull at her she remembered Brookenham talking about not needing an heir, that he had cousins who could fulfill that obligation. Yet, surely this was more than an heir. It was his child. Their child.

The man hadn't even asked after her health. There seemed to be no concern. No worry. No understanding of the fear coursing through her. It all seemed so cold.

She pulled a cotton handkerchief from her pocket and wiped both eyes.

"My Lady?" Maggie said from behind her as she came into the room. The obvious concern in her voice told Isobel that the maid had seen her crying.

She sniffed and quickly hid the handkerchief in her pocket. There was no need for the staff to see how upset she was.

"Mister Wesley asked me to remind you," Maggie began, "that the Church council is due to arrive in a few hours."

Isobel sighed and glanced out the window one last time as James turned onto the road. He did not look back over his shoulder, she thought, as another wave of sadness washed over her. No of course not.

Was he already thinking of the women of London? Already planning out his next conquest? Mentally cataloging and evaluating the widows and wantons of the ton. Or, would he go for an actress perhaps? Someone who made no demands.

Would he focus his attention on one, or would there be a multitude? Her heart ached at the thought. She knew her husband. He would not be lonely. Of that, there was no doubt. Women would be lined up to share his bed.

Her stomach clenched up in despair as once again tears began to roll down her cheek.

She must pull herself together, she realized. There were things to do and people to help. People with real problems. No, there was no time to wallow in self-pity. Turning to Maggie, she put on her best smile and said, "Please tell

Wesley that I will meet them in here. We have already discussed the light luncheon to be served."

"Of course, Ma'am," Maggie said as she dropped a quick curtsy and left to do as she was instructed.

Isobel turned back to the window, unable to stop from staring out into the world. There were so many things to regret. She wondered which she would miss the most. Their nights together in his bed? The way he laughed easily at her jokes? No, she realized. It would be those quiet moments over the chess table. Where he treated her as a formable opponent. An equal.

She would miss those quiet moments alone with the man she loved.

Chapter Twenty-Three

Lord Brookenham looked out over the dance floor and slowly shook his head. These people had no idea of the danger they faced. He wondered if it had been like this in France before the revolution.

The high and mighty leading their lives while all the time, hate and discontent bubbled below them.

It was as if they were dancing on high wires over a boiling caldron. Completely unaware that one false step and everything would collapse.

He had spent the last month talking and listening to everyone he could find who was willing to talk. Mostly he listened. From farm hands to publicans. Vicars to grandmothers. He had talked to any and every one.

Things needed to change or things would explode. Not a lot, but enough to give people hope. Yes, the mills needed wool. But throwing tenants off of farms to convert the land to pasture could not be the answer. Keeping corn prices high for the benefit of the landlords was pushing the people to hate the nobility.

The King's madness had helped start the questions. If the King was mad, then had he truly been chosen by God to rule? And if not, then who should? Then, Prinny's scandals had only highlighted the distance between the average person and the nobility that ruled them.

Of course, the war with Napoleon had been costly in both treasure and men. Too many families had lost a loved one on some foreign field or to the deep blue sea. A soul that would never return to them.

No, it was surprising things had not already exploded.

Sighing, he turned away as his mind fought to develop some kind of solution. Something that would convince the necessary people of the need for reform.

Unfortunately, that would mean people giving up some control. Some privileges, perhaps some wealth. Impossible. But they needed to see that if they didn't give up a little now, they would lose it all later.

"Lord Brookenham," Lady Burton said as she walked towards him. His insides tightened up. This was the woman that had helped Darlington compromise Isobel. It was surprising that she had the gall to address him in public.

But, then what should he expect from a Lady of the ton. Nothing really mattered. Everything was fair game. Self-awareness was not their strong point.

"Lady Burton," he replied without smiling.

She balked for a moment as she realized he was still upset with her. But, being the kind of woman she was, she continued on as if nothing had occurred.

"I must say that I am not surprised at your return. Domesticity is not in your nature."

His brow furrowed in a deep frown. What did she mean by that?

"I was sorry to hear that your young bride had remained at Brookenham," she continued. "So many people wish to learn how she landed such a catch as yourself."

He snorted, she lied very well. Of course, she was pleased with Isobel's absence. That would be one less beauty for her to compete with. But her statement about people talking about their marriage was obviously true. He himself had heard the rumors.

"My Dear Dear wife is in the middle of redecorating Brookenham," he said. "I've given her carte blanche. She is completely engrossed."

There, that should hurt a little. Lady Burton had always thought of herself as a setter of style. The thought of some other women designing the interior of Brookenham would not sit well with her.

Her eyes flashed for the briefest of seconds. Yes, he thought, he had scored a solid point. But not near as much as this woman deserved for trying to hurt Isobel. No, he would have to think of something else.

"Oh, I am sure she will be able to use her rustic charm to excellent effect," She said with just a hint of disdain.

He ignored her as he turned to look out over the crowd. From the corner of his eye, he caught her staring up at him, obviously dying for him to ask her to dance.

"If you will excuse me," he said, "I need to find Norwich."

Her eyes registered a brief disappointment before she quickly hid the look and smiled sweetly.

"Of course, I believe I saw him in the far corner talking to Lord Wheaton."

He nodded and left her without a formal goodbye.

Things had changed, he realized. A few months ago he would have asked her to dance and then spent the night seducing the young widow. He had seen it in her eyes. She had been more than willing.

But there had always been something more with Lady Burton. It had always been rather obvious that she hoped to be his wife. Yet now, that look, was she telling him she was willing to be his mistress?

He snorted. Once again, a woman trying to use him for her own benefit.

But no longer. Women like Lady Burton left him feeling empty. Cold.

Sighing, he shook his head as he wove through the crowd to find Norwich alone in the far corner.

"I can't take much more of this," Norwich said. "I'm returning to Ann in the morning. Cambridge has already left."

"You can't," Brookenham said. "We aren't there yet."

Norwich shrugged. "They won't listen to me. I've burnt too many bridges over the years. And Cambridge?" he scoffed. "They think his years in America have tainted him. Everything he says is twisted and turned against him."

Brookenham sighed. Norwich was right. The other Lords refused to listen to them.

"But you," Norwich said as he clapped him on the back. "They listen to you."

Again, Brookenham sighed, no matter how much he hoped his friend was correct, he doubted it.

"No," Norwich continued. "They can see your passion. They respect your command of the facts. No, you must keep trying. You will sway them eventually."

Lord Brookenham's shoulders slumped. It was unfair. His friends were returning to their wives. Yet he was to remain here in London. The thought seemed wrong on so many levels. He was the newlywed. The other two couples had been married for years and should have long ago become accustomed to being separated.

But no, it was to be him that remained. Of course, everyone knew his marriage was but a convenience. Not true love. Therefore, it cost him nothing to remain in London.

"Of course," he told Norwich. "I will continue to try to convince them. But I doubt I will be successful."

"Small steps," Norwich told him. "Remember, every step leads us away from catastrophe."

Brookenham nodded, his friend was correct. But that did not mean he was going to enjoy it.

But then, why not. ? He had nothing more important. His wife was content, safely ensconced at Brookenham. This had been the agreement. She would have a family, the estate, a staff of servants. He would have London and the rest of Britain.

He took a deep breath and let the weight of the world settle on his shoulders.

Sighing internally, he thought back six years and could only scoff at how things had changed. At twenty, his future had been so bright. A life of comfort, little responsibility. Nights of debauchery.

A British gentleman. But then without warning he had been lifted to the life of a British Lord. Thrust into a life of responsibility and status. He had adjusted, taken to his new role because that was what was expected.

Then, the surprise of all. Marriage to Miss Isobel Stafford. He could only shake his head. He had never seen that coming. And now. To be a father. Again, never in his plans. The thought made his insides turn over.

What did he know about being a father?

And now. Dukes and Earls wanted him to lead the way in convincing stodgy British Lords to change their customs. To vote against their interests.

The weight of it all felt like a load of bricks. Always present, always pulling at him.

"You will do well," Norwich said as he slapped him on the back once again. "And remember, when you begin to believe it is too much, remember that coal miner digging through the muck so his family might eat that night. Or the crofter walking behind a plow. Wishing with every step that he could be anywhere else. Remember, life could be so much worse."

Brookenham laughed. As always, his friend was right. No, he had no room for complaint. Yet, that did not remove the ache in the bottom of his stomach at the thought of Isobel and the cold bed waiting for him at home.

Yes, life could be worse. But it would never be as good as it should have been.

.oOo.

Isobel ran her hand over her tummy and wondered about the child. When would she begin to show? When would she feel the baby move? These and a thousand other questions filled her mind every waking moment.

It seemed she was always thinking about the baby. Either that or her husband. Where was he now? she wondered. And with whom.

Did he think of her?

An ache filled her heart as she stared out the parlor window. Three weeks. The man had been gone for three weeks and the pain had not diminished in any way.

Oh, why had she allowed herself to fall in love? It would have been so much easier if they had maintained their emotional distance. That formal acceptance of each other's existence. Instead, she had allowed her feeling to blossom and expand until she could think of nothing but James.

What a fool she had been. A shudder ran down her spine as she thought about how stupid she had been. A silly school girl who had fallen for a strong, commanding man. She had filled every cliché.

Sighing, she began to return to her seat when a distant movement caught her eye. A coach, turning onto the drive. For a brief moment, her heart jumped at the thought that James might be returning. Only for her spirits to crash at the memory that the family coach remained in the barn.

If James were to return, it would be on the back of his favorite horse.

Who? she wondered as she watched the carriage pull to a stop. Then she couldn't help but smile as her sister, Lydia, stepped down from the carriage, then turned to receive a baby from the nurse's arms.

Isobel's heart soared as she ran from the parlor and out the front door just as Wesley greeted their guest.

"Welcome, Your Grace," Wesley said as he bowed at the waist. Lydia blushed slightly. It seemed even her sister hadn't grown used to be addressed by her title.

"Lydia," Isobel said as she rushed past the butler to give her sister a fierce hug. This was so perfect, exactly who she needed.

"Where is Johnathon?" Isobel asked as she glanced into the coach looking for her favorite nephew.

"With Cambridge," Lydia answered. "He and Gray Wolf threatened to take the boy hunting with them. I managed to get them to comprise and agree to a fishing trip instead."

Isobel's heart stopped. "Your husband has returned from London?"

Lydia nodded as she stepped into the house. "Yes, and Norwich has returned to Ann. He refuses to be away from her as her time grows near."

"They both left London?"

Her sister nodded confirmation then said, "It seems Brookenham volunteered to lead their cause."

Isobel froze in her steps. What had she expected? Of course, he had remained. Her heart hurt as she fought to push away the pain.

Of course. Politics and London were more important to him than his wife and child. Why had she ever expected anything different?

Chapter Twenty-Four

Isobel rocked Little Thomas as Lydia and Aunt Ester talked over their tea. Smiling down at the boy she couldn't help but wonder about what it would feel like to hold her own child.

"So?" Lydia said when she had finished with her Aunt. That was so Lydia, Isobel thought. Always considerate. Always perfectly mannered.

"A child," her sister said with a smirk. "Really, Isobel, that was rather quick."

Isobel couldn't help but blush as she shrugged, what was she supposed to say to such a statement.

"I must say," Lydia continued, "both Ann and I were shocked to hear about your wedding. Especially when it was rushed so quickly that neither of your sisters could attend. But to learn you were increasing so soon. I will gather that there are a great many tongues wagging in London."

Isobel's stomach dropped when she said it like that. It really did cast things in the worst light.

"I do apologize about the wedding," Isobel said. "Brookenham insisted we be married immediately."

Lydia's brow furrowed for a moment, "Really. Since when did my sister acquiesce to James Brookenham. We always believed you two were arch enemies. Then to hear that you had been wed. Both Ann and I were quite surprised."

"Enemies?" Aunt Ester interjected. "These two were never enemies."

Isobel felt her world slipping away. The last thing she wanted to talk about was the relationship with her husband.

"You didn't see them in London," Lydia said to their Aunt with a shake of her head. "I do believe they never exchanged a civil word. Ann and I used to have to work to keep them apart."

"Really Lydia," Isobel said with a huff. "It was never that bad."

Her sister arched an eyebrow then took another sip of her tea.

"And now, I must say your letter was a shock. To discover that my little sister is with child. It is rather disturbing. I was pleased, of course. But surprised."

A small anger began to build inside of Isobel as she stared at Lydia. "I am not a little girl. I am a married woman after all. It should not be that shocking."

Lydia shrugged, "yes, but Lord Brookenham? Now Lord Darlington, I could understand. He seems like such a better match for you."

"What?" Isobel exclaimed. "You would never understand. Besides. Brookenham is an excellent husband. He is kind, generous, intelligent. And very brave. What more could a woman want?"

Her sister bit back a small smile as she took another sip of her tea. Turning to her Aunt, Lydia's smile grew as she nodded.

"You were correct," she told the older woman. "She has fallen in love with him."

"WHAT?" Isobel said so loudly that the baby in her armed startled and looked up at her with a cross expression, obviously upset at having his nap disturbed.

"What?" she said to her sister more softly.

Lydia laughed, "Aunt Ester wrote to me. It is nothing to be ashamed of Isobel. A wife should fall in love with their husbands. It makes life so much easier. I assure you."

Isobel sighed heavily as her heart tore in two. "But only if they love them back. Otherwise, it is pure misery."

Lydia grimaced as her eyes softened. "I am sorry, but I wouldn't worry. He will come around. I promise."

"I don't think so," Isobel said. "Not as long as he is in London and I am here. No. I do not believe I am to have the happiness you and Ann have both found."

Her sister's expression said it all. She felt sorry for her sister. What woman wouldn't?

Sighing heavily. Isobel pushed it behind her and returned to rocking her nephew. Focus on the future she thought. Focus on what she had not what she would never have.

Lydia stayed only two days then insisted she had to return home. Isobel could not blame her. The woman had a family. A loving husband. Of course, she would want to be with them.

"You will be fine," Lydia told her as she prepared to enter the coach. "Your doctor is surprisingly intelligent, and even more important, your midwife is very experienced. The staff are supportive. I promise, everything will go well. I will come back as you get closer. Perhaps Ann will be able to travel by then."

Isobel smiled. The thought of having both her sisters there meant a great deal. Nothing bad could happen if they were together.

"Bring Johnathon," she told Lydia. "I would like him to meet his new cousin."

Lydia smiled then gave her a long hug before stepping up into the carriage.

"And Isobel," she said as she leaned out the window, "when Brookenham comes back. Let him catch you. That is who he is. A hero at heart. Let him be one."

Isobel winced, the thought of her husband brought with it pain and regret. But she had no choice but to smile and nod as if her sister's advice was readably accepted.

Sighing to herself, she watched the coach turn onto the main road then returned inside. Once again alone.

Except for the baby, she thought as her hand gently rubbed her stomach.

Slowly over the next few weeks, she fell into a routine, rising late. A large breakfast. A walk in the orchard. Meetings with the staff. Or with the women working on the draperies. The project had been expanded to include all of the bed linen throughout the house.

If the weather was inclement, she would find a book and try to pass the time.

A quiet dinner served in the parlor. The dining room was too large, too formal. It made her feel even more alone.

No, she would have a quiet meal, then eventually retire upstairs only to repeat everything the next day.

Slowly, days became weeks and weeks became months.

As the baby grew, she came to think of it as a him. It would be a boy, and she would name him James after his father. Her heart melted as she thought of the child and what he would become. Tall, strong like his father. Intelligent and caring. The kind of man a mother could be proud of.

A sense of contentment filled her. She and the baby had grown to know each other's moods. During the day while she was active, he would sleep, constantly growing. At night, while she rested, he preferred to be up and about. Moving inside of her, never letting her get a full night's rest.

In the middle of her seventh month. Just as she thought she was becoming accustomed to this new life. She was visited by very strong headaches. A dull, pounding pain that seemed to block out half her vision. Narrowing her eyesight to a small tunnel before her.

On those days, she remained in bed with one candle burning in the far corner. Maggie would check on her. The maid's face twisted with concern as she brought in a tray of light food.

Knowing that she must eat to keep up her strength and for the health of the baby, Isobel would nibble at the food on the tray then turn over and try to become lost in the darkness.

"Here, My Lady," Maggie said after a particularly bad morning. "I had Cook make you some willow bark tea. My mother swore by it."

Isobel tried to smile her appreciation as she forced herself to sit up in bed and sip at the bitter concoction.

Turning up her nose she shook her head. "No wonder your mother got better. If just so that she could avoid drinking this."

Maggie laughed as she gathered her mistress's clothes for washing.

"You must finish it, My Lady," she said with a bundle of clothes in her arms.

Isobel sighed as it was obvious the maid would not leave until she had finished.

Setting her shoulders, she took a deep breath and finished the drink. Then tipped the cup so that Maggie could see that it was all gone.

The maid smiled and nodded before she left.

The same ritual was completed the next morning and the morning after that.

On the fourth morning, Isobel sank back onto the bed only to eventually realize that the tea had worked. Her headache was gone. Or at least far enough away that it could be ignored.

Yes, she thought as a sense of energy filled her. Yes, she must be up and off. There were a dozen things that needed to be addressed. She needed to inspect the work on the nursery. She needed to meet with Mrs. Carter about the project. They needed to finalize the cloth selection for His Lordship's study for one.

This and a hundred other thoughts flashed through her mind as she swung her legs over the side of the bed.

"Well James," she said as she rubbed her stomach. "Which shall we do first. The nursery?"

The baby kicked, obviously pleased to be out of bed and moving about.

She had taken only two steps towards the wash basin when a massive cramp gripped her about the middle. Reaching out she caught the back of a chair to stop herself from falling.

"My Lady," Maggie yelled as she rushed into the room.

"Help me back to bed," Isobel croaked as a terrifying fear filled her. No. Not now. It was not time.

"Here My Lady," Maggie said as she slipped under Isobel's arm and half carried her back to the bed.

Isobel's mind whirled as she desperately fought to understand what was going on. It was too soon. Her skin tingled and her insides threatened to rebel.

"Should I send for the doctor?" Maggie asked with a terrified expression on her face.

"No, I will be fine," Isobel said as she breathed through her teeth, fighting to make the fear go away.

Maggie frowned for a long moment then gasped. "My Lady," she said with eyes as big as toadstools. "You shift," she added as she pointed to the front of Isobel's white cotton nightgown.

Isobel's brow furrowed as she looked down to examine her shift. Her heart froze as every terror she had ever known filled her.

The white cotton was stained with a small blotch of red.

"Get the Doctor," she hissed to Maggie as another cramp took hold.

Chapter Twenty-Five

Lord Brookenham glanced at his cards and sighed internally. Another night discussing politics at White's. Somehow his life had taken a twist he had never anticipated.

Slow progress, he reminded himself as he played his card. Lord Devonshire seemed to be open-minded about things. Unlike his father, at least the man would listen without instantly dismissing him.

"So, Brookenham," Lord Wheaton began as he played his card. "I ..." the older Lord stopped suddenly as his brow furrowed for a moment while he looked over Lord Brookenham's shoulder.

The young Earl shifted to turn and see what Wheaton was looking at. His stomach dropped as he recognized John, his footman, approaching with a very concerned expression on his face.

He instantly recalled his last words to Isobel. He was but a day away, if she needed him, send John. For the briefest moment, his heart jumped. She had sent for him. Then seeing the concern in John's eyes, his heart slammed to an instant stop.

"What is it?" he asked the footman.

"Mr. Wesley sent me, My Lord."

Again, a quick shaft of pain flashed through him. "How is Lady Brookenham? The baby? Tell me."

John swallowed hard and said, "Mr. Wesley said to say, Sir, that the Doctor wishes for you to hurry. Time is of the essence."

Brookenham's blood ran cold. "It is more than the baby. Her Ladyship?"

The footman swallowed hard, unable to meet his stare.

Lord Brookenham's world stopped spinning for the briefest moment. Isobel? the baby. No, it was too soon. They were in danger. Every fiber of his being cried out to protect them. He had failed. Instead of being with her, watching over her. He had been playing cards.

Of all the stupid, idiotic, pursuits, he thought as he pushed past the footman without a word to his table companions.

Once outside, he hailed a cab and rushed home.

"Saddle my horse," he yelled as he ran upstairs to change. Isobel! it was all he could think about. He needed to get there as quickly as possible. As he hurriedly changed out of his evening clothes, he mentally mapped out his route. Which Inns would be the best place to switch horses? Which back road could provide the best shortcut?

Within a dozen minutes of being told that he was needed at home, Lord Brookenham stepped up onto his horse and was off without a backward glance.

As he raced through the dark streets of London, he forced himself to hold the stallion back less it slip on the cobblestones. But once clear of the city, he leaned forward and let the beast loose.

While the pounding of the horse's hooves became lost in the night. Brookenham's mind wandered to a thousand different scenarios. Each one worse that the other.

Wesley would not have sent for him unless it was dire. And why hadn't Isobel sent for him? Was she already too far gone? In fact, even now, his wife might be dead and he not even know it. The thought sent a cold chill running down his back.

How could he have been so wrong. He should never have left her there all alone.

Even if she had pushed him away. She was his wife. His responsibility. He should never have left her. A sick, sour feeling filled him. It was too early for the baby. Could it even survive if it came this early? What of Isobel? Surely, she could survive?

As the horse rounded a wide bend in the road, Brookenham glanced up at the silvery moon and offered up a quick prayer of thanks. Without it, he could never have taken this road at a full gallop at night.

No sooner had the thought occurred than the horse stumbled. It's lead foot slipping in a patch of mud.

A flash of panic filled him. If he fell now, it would be days before he got home. If he didn't kill himself first.

Brookenham gripped with his knees as he urged the horse to find himself. The animal floundered for a brief second then regained his footing and once again was off. Brookenham sighed. Keep your focus, he reminded himself. It would do no one any good if he got killed this night.

Taking a deep breath, he pulled back on the reins just slightly. Enough to slow the racing beast but not enough to significantly affect his pace. The two of them settled into a pattern. Brookenham nodded to himself. Yes, the horse could keep this up long enough to reach the stables he intended to use.

Of course, once he got to the Inn, he had to yell to wake the stableman. You would think an Inn this close to London would know to expect late night business.

As he and the new horse raced through the night, he let his mind wander to visions of Isobel. He had missed her, he realized. Truly missed her. Not just her body, but the woman herself.

The thought made him scoff to himself. Who would ever have believed that he could come to miss Isobel Stafford of all people? But it was true. These last six months since he had returned to London had shown him just what she had come to mean to him.

Of course, the realization did him no good. The woman no longer needed him. That had been rather evident in the short, cold notes he had received once a month.

An anger began to build inside of him. Granted, she had never wished to be married to him. But that did not change the fact that she was his wife.

The thought sent a coldness through him. Only if she was still alive, he realized.

As he raced up the drive to his home, he was surprised to see every window lit like a mid-winter's party. The entire household must be up and about he thought as he jumped from his horse and tossed the reins to Jack, the stableman.

The look of concern on the old man's face filled Brookenham with a bone gnawing fear. The deep furrow on Wesley's brow confirmed it. Things were not going well.

"Her Ladyship?" he barked at the butler as he rushed past him.

"I don't know, My Lord," the Butler replied. "The Doctor and the midwife are with her now."

As Brookenham turned to rush up the stairs, a high-pitched wail from Isobel's room sent a shaft of pure terror to his very soul.

"Isobel," he whispered under his breath as he began to race up the stairs. The sound echoed in his mind. She was in pain. Awful, terrible pain.

Before he could reach the door, Maggie, his wife's maid stepped out, her eyebrows rising to her hairline when she saw the Earl rushing towards her.

"My Lord," the young woman said as she held out her hand to stop him, giving him a fierce look of determination. "Not now. She wouldn't want you to see her like this."

"I don't care what she wants," he yelled as he started to push past the young maid.

"I do!" Maggie said as she stepped in front him blocking his way.

Brookenham stared down at the young woman, shocked to have someone trying to stop him. While he had never physically attacked a woman, if she didn't move, now would be the first time.

"My Lord," Maggie said with a calming voice. "You will only make things worse."

Brookenham froze. Was Maggie right? Would he make things worse? What would he do anyway? There were no enemies to defeat. No mountains to conquer. The realization of just

261

how helpless he was filled him with hopelessness and fear.

No, if he couldn't help her. He could at least not make things worse.

Seeing that he had regained some sense, Maggie sighed and said, "I will send the doctor out."

He took a deep breath and nodded. She stared at him for a moment, obviously trying to judge whether she could trust him to remain outside. Then seemed to make up her mind and quickly slipped back into the room. The young woman was so quick he couldn't get a good look inside.

Turning, he began to pace the hallway outside his wife's door. Like men for thousands of years before him, He could only wait and worry.

At last, the doctor came out, wiping his hands on a towel and frowned as he slowly shook his head.

"What? Damn it," Brookenham said as he took the man by the shoulders and held him in place.

The doctor sighed. "I don't know. The baby is early. Very early. She, Her Ladyship is not … ready. Things are not going well."

Brookenham's insides froze solid as the realization of just what might happen finally settled in. Women died during childbirth all the time. This was real. No longer a concept, or possibility. He could lose her.

"What can I do?" Brookenham asked the doctor as he stared into the man's eyes.

The doctor stared back then said, "Pray."

The Earl swallowed hard as he realized that deep down, the Doctor did not expect his wife or child to make it. That by the morn, he would be a widower.

As the doctor turned and went back into Isobel's room, Brookenham winced as he heard his wife grunt in pain.

"Please," he begged as he looked up to the heavens. "Tell me, and it is yours."

The deadly silence filled him with a helplessness.

"Anything," he whispered. "Church, every Sunday. I promise. What else?"

Again, more silence.

"Please," he begged. "Let her live."

But there was no indication that his plea had been heard. Nothing.

Sighing, he began to pace, his movement only halting when another cry of pain echoed from the room.

It seemed to go on forever. This strange purgatory. Maids would rush from the room to retrieve something or other. Each time, shooting him frightened looks. Each time, his heart would break into smaller pieces.

It took every bit of will to stop himself from crashing into her room. He didn't know if he could continue like this when there was a particularly strong scream followed by silence.

He froze as the sudden quiet engulfed him. What had happened? Why wouldn't someone come tell him? Did Isobel need him? Would he even have an opportunity to say goodbye?

As his hand reached for the knob, a sudden high-pitched cry made him freeze. That wasn't Isobel. No, it was a baby's cry.

His hand froze above the doorknob as a new fear washed through him. What if the baby lived but he lost Isobel? How was he supposed to raise a child on his own? No, the baby needed his mother. No, he needed his wife. It could not be allowed to happen.

Pushing aside the fear, he stepped into the room to so see his wife's angelic face looking at him with a sense of bliss and happiness. The baby, wrapped in swaddling clothes lying in her arms.

"James," she said with a smile that melted his heart. "You came?"

He froze, unable to believe what he was seeing. This woman he loved more than life itself holding his child. His world shifted as he realized that things would never be the same again. For the first time in his life, he realized what was truly important.

Family. Love. Hope.

"Isobel," he whispered. Their eyes locked as he slowly made his way to her.

She smiled up at him, then down at their child. "Your son," she said indicating the baby. "I thought we would call him James. He looks like you."

The Earl's insides turned over as he stared down at his son. The boy was so small, red faced, and squirming. Brookenham's heart grew three sizes to take in all the love he felt at that moment.

It was impossible to pull his stare away from the child. He looked so tiny. So helpless. Isobel adjusted herself as she smiled at the maids and Doctor.

"Thank You," she said to them as they dipped their heads and slowly left to give them a moment together. Only Maggie remained, standing in the corner, ready if she was needed.

Isobel looked up at Brookenham and frowned slightly.

"What is wrong?" he asked as his heart jumped.

"Nothing," she said with a slight shake of her head.

He sighed heavily. "Isobel," he began. "We cannot keep doing this. Strangers, sharing nothing but a child. You must agree to tell me what you are thinking."

She studied him for a long moment, her brow furrowed in confusion.

"You first," she said, obviously unwilling to open herself to him.

He took a deep breath. The night had been filled with many fears. But this one he could overcome.

Laughing to himself, he shook his head and said, "What am I thinking? If you must know. I have fallen in love with you and wish to have a normal marriage. No longer these separate lives. I want to raise our children together. I want to come home and be able to tell you about my day.

Her face grew as white as the sheets she lay beneath and he knew that he had pushed things too far and too fast. He had hoped that at this moment, she might feel a little for him.

"Brookenham," she said as she reached out and took his hand. Staring up into his eyes she smiled the most contented smile any new mother had ever had.

"I have loved you since the first time I saw you. I tried to believe it was but a silly school girl's crush. But it has grown into so much more. My love for you consumes me.

Her words hit him like an avalanche, burying him beneath a thousand thoughts and emotions. She did love him. Just as he loved her.

Looking at her, then at his son, Lord Brookenham knew that his life would be filled with joy and happiness. It would be a life with meaning. How could it not, with Miss Isobel Stafford by his side?

Epilogue

Isobel bounced little Ester on her hip as she watched James and his cousins race across the lawn.

Ann was rocking Beatrice and smiled at her sister with a smile of pure contentment.

Lydia stepped up between them and pulled them both into a quick hug.

"Who would ever have thought," she said as she nodded at the children playing tag.

Aunt Ester, who was standing on the other side of Ann laughed, "I don't know, with men like that," she said as she nodded to the three tall men standing off to the side discussing horses. "Of course, you lot would have a great many children."

The three sisters each blushed but there was no denying the fact. That each of them had married viral, strong men. Men who loved them. Men that made a woman want to have a family.

Isobel smiled to herself. Of course, getting there was half the fun.

As she stared at her husband, he seemed to feel her watching him and looked up. Catching her stare, he smiled knowingly. It was there. The one they shared when the rest of the world disappeared and it was just the two of them.

Two people in love.

The End

Author's Notes

Thank you for reading 'The Very British Lord.' The second third in the 'Stafford Sisters' series.

I would love to know what you think of it. My readers make it possible for me to do what I love so I am always grateful and excited to hear from you. Please stop by my website GLSnodgrass.com or send me an Email at GL@GLSnodgrass.com. Feel free to sign up for my newsletter. I use my newsletter to announce new releases and give away free books. I also post on my Facebook page. https://www.facebook.com/G.L.Snodgrass/

As always, I would like to thank my friends for their assistance with this book. Sheryl Turner, Anya Monroe, Eryn Carpenter, and Kim Loraine. I couldn't have done it without them.

If you enjoyed 'The Very British Lord' please tell a friend or two. And please help out by rating this book at Amazon, Bookbub, or Goodreads. Reviews from readers make a huge difference for a writer.

I have also included the first two chapters to my book The Reluctant Duke, the first book in the 'Love's Pride' series.

Again, thank you.

The Reluctant Duke
Prologue

Wet cobblestones echoed with the slap of her bare feet as the cold night air bit through her thin cotton nightgown. Turning and peering through the fog the young woman searched to see if she was followed. Her heart raced, beating so loud she was sure they would hear.

 Was that movement, had they found her already? With a stomach turned to stone, she fled. Where in this town would ever be safe? How truly alone she was flashed through her mind as she tried to think of someone to help.

There was no one. No one powerful enough to stop him. London was lost to her.

Chapter One

Duty is like a double-edged sword hanging over a man's neck. It dictates everything.

Major Thomas Marshal's horse slowly walked up the long path towards his new home. It had been a long ride from London. His back ached, and his leg screamed in protest.

"God, it's worse than I thought," he said to himself as he looked over the dark and imposing building.

Dead flower beds and fallen tree limbs made the area look like a neglected step-child. Chipped bricks, a broken window on one of the upper floors, at least a dozen little things showed significant neglect.

His stomach turned over with the thought of what lay before him.

Brookshire! At least one Prime Minister and two pirates had been born here. Kings and Queens had dined at its table. This old palatial estate was known throughout the Kingdom and most of Europe as the home of the Duke of Bathurst. Center of a vast estate with properties throughout Britain and the continent.

Squaring his shoulders, he sat tall in his saddle and waited. No one came out to greet him, no stable boy appeared to take his horse, and no footman in full livery scurried down the front steps.

"What's the meaning of this," he wondered aloud as his stomach turned over with the first inkling of worry. Sighing, he gingerly swung down from his horse and limped up the steps using his cane to rap against the heavy oaken door.

He paused, he waited. Still, no one arrived. Heaving a heavy sigh again and shaking his head he slowly opened the door and crossed the threshold.

The house was huge. It always had been. Built-in Elizabethan times with that typical Tudor thirst for function and efficiency. A memory of getting lost in the upper floors when he had been very young flashed through his mind. Of sliding down the banister when no one watched. There had been a few good things.

Glass windows allowed enough light to examine his surroundings. Solid English oak greeted him wherever he looked. Brown, a lot of brown, just like he remembered it. Clean, but old. Well-worn and showing its age.

Still, no one came to greet him. The place was as empty as a mausoleum. The butler or footmen should be scurrying to take care of his needs. That tense feeling at the bottom of his belly didn't go away. He could remember the house having dozens of staff, people to take care of every wish and whim of the old bastard.

A slight movement down the far hall caught his attention. Leaning on his cane, Thomas limped across the hardwood entryway where he spotted the prettiest rump he'd seen in a long time. A maid on her hands and knees was scrubbing the floor. Her beautiful rear end draped in a gray maid's uniform shifted back and forth as she scoured with a brush.

"Freddy, if you tracked mud over my clean floor, I will butcher you alive," the young maid said while she continued to push the brush back and forth across the floor.

He looked back to ensure he hadn't tracked in any mud. He was able to relax when he saw a dirt free path behind him. Standing there, Thomas admired the view.

The young woman stopped scrubbing and looked over her shoulder then squealed.

"I'm sorry sir," she said rising and giving a quick curtsy. "Can I help you? His Grace is not at home," she added.

The Major examined the woman in front of him. Her face was flushed with exertion or embarrassment. Her hands were red and raw from the cold water and harsh lye. Even so, she was a very pretty little thing.

A stray blond strand of hair fell from her cap. Her dress was wet to the knees, and her sleeves were pushed up to exposed two graceful arms. A pity she was totally and completely forbidden to him. A deep regret passed through him at the thought.

"I am the new 'His Grace,'" he answered.

The look of pure shock and opened mouth surprise on the maid's pretty face almost made him smile.

"Please have the butler, housekeeper, and Cook join me in the study."

Years of training had created an expert at hiding emotions. The last thing he was going to do was show the servants what he was feeling. Instead, he turned and slowly walked to what used to be his Grandfather's study.

Thomas Marshall, His Grace, the Fourth Duke of Bathurst, Third Viscount of Readly, Baron Von Trolst of Saxony and former Major of Her Majesty's Coldstream Regiment of Foot sat at his Grandfather's desk completely lost and unsure of himself. A rather strange and unusual feeling.

His stomach rebelled at the thought of what he was about to take on. The soul-crushing responsibility and the complete abandonment of any chance at peace.

Placing both hands palm down on the desk he looked out over the room. He was never supposed to be here. Not in this room, not in this chair. His eyes cataloged the contents of the room as he took in the moldy smells of leather, paper, and musty rugs. Sighing he relaxed his shoulders.

"Duty," he mumbled to himself while shaking his head.

Six months ago he'd been lying in a field hospital with a French bullet in his leg. Nine years of fighting in Egypt, across the Peninsula, through France, and into Belgium and he's wounded on the last day of the last battle of the war.

Laying there on the straw in that pest-ridden hospital, he'd thought that fighting with the doctors over whether to amputate or not had been the toughest thing he'd ever have to face. He now knew there were harder mountains to climb.

A soft knock at the door and the pretty maid stepped in followed by what appeared to be a very young footman and an older, heavyset woman he remembered as the cook.

"Yes?" he said, waiting patiently.

"Excuse me, Your Grace," said the pretty maid, her gaze shifting back and forth between her companions and then to him.

His breath hitched, what eyes, he hadn't realized how striking they were. The deepest blue, almost violet. They brought color and beauty to the world. What is this woman doing here as a maid? Her face, her figure, those eyes! She could command any price, demand any conditions and most men would bend to her wishes just to possess her. He was so nonplussed that he missed her first few words

"... tell you earlier, the Butler, Mr. Evans and the housekeeper Mrs. Fischer left over three months ago," She said looking down at her feet. Once she was done she quietly backed up to join the other two servants.

He got up from the desk and limped towards them, resting his weight on the damn walking stick.

"What do you mean, they left. Where'd they go?" he asked, dumbfounded. There had been no mention of this at the solicitor's office yesterday.

"They eloped, sir."

"What!" The Major turned Duke barked.

"Yes sir," The young maid said, cringing.

"Well, they didn't have to leave. I'm sure they could have continued, even as a married couple … Um, I assume that they eloped with each other that is."

"Yes sir, but I don't think that's why they left sir," she said, raising her eyes to meet his.

"You don't, then why did they leave, and …" suddenly realizing something, "Where's the rest of the staff," he asked, not wanting to hear the answer.

"They also left, in fact, the Butler Mr. Evans, told them too, sir."

"He did? Why?"

He looked at the two other staff members trying to gauge the validity of what he was being told. Each of them nodded, confirming his worst fears. Clenching his jaw, he returned to concentrating on what she was saying. He had to fight with himself to not get lost in those eyes.

"Mr. Evans told them that if they weren't going to get paid, they didn't have to stay and that they should look for other arrangements. In fact, he prepared letters of recommendations for each of the staff, sir."

She didn't cringe at all, well not much. He'd been told that he could intimidate a bear. Seasoned sergeants had quaked at the thought of bringing him bad news. She wouldn't have been the first to tremble. Instead, she'd looked him square in the face and told him his staff had deserted because they hadn't been properly taken care of.

The fact that he hadn't known that he even had a staff was beside the point and did not solve the issue.

He'd met with the solicitors and bankers in London immediately upon returning from France. They'd shown him the accounts. There was more money than Midas ever dreamed of. Granted, most of it was all tied up in court and land and what not. But there should have been more than enough to pay the staff. Obviously, there wasn't anyone here to oversee the minor detail of ensuring people got paid.

A wave of guilt swept over him.

Putting it aside to deal with later, he reminded himself that what he thought was important might not be viewed the same way in some London banker's office.

Running a hand through his hair, he studied the maid's two companions. "Mrs. Morgan? Isn't it?"

"Yes Your Grace," the cook replied with a small curtsy.

"I remember your excellent raspberry tarts."

The large woman smiled and blushed obviously surprised that he would remember after all these years.

"And you sir," he addressed the young footman. "You must be the famous 'Freddy' I've heard so much about." This time, the pretty maid blushed slightly.

"Yes Sir, Freddy Goodwin, sir," he said as he bowed at the waist.

"Well Goodwin, fix your top button and then take my horse to the stable and have ..., do we have any stable hands?"

"Yes sir, Old Jack, is still here," he said, his fingers shaking as he fixed his top button.

"Then have 'Old Jack' care for my horse, I'll be out to check on him later."

"Right away Your Grace," Freddy said, looking relieved to be able to escape.

"And you are?" The new Duke asked the pretty maid

"Gwen, Your Grace," she answered, giving a quick curtsy.

Was that a hesitant answer, he wondered, and that curtsy. He studied her closely, her intelligence was obvious, and she sounded educated. Not at all like a common downstairs maid.

While he didn't have a lot of experience with pretty maids, something wasn't right. She didn't shy away, but she wasn't forthcoming with information either. Her ability to look him in the eye and hold his stare was unusual, but then everything around here was unusual.

"Well Gwen, Mrs. Morgan, What's been going on here?" He asked,

The two women looked at each other; Mrs. Morgan said, "Sir, I have a meat pie that is due to come out of the oven, and I was hoping to start some raspberry tarts. I'm sure that Gwen here can answer all of your questions. She's been taking care of everything since that bas... I am sorry, since Mr. Evans left."

"Of course Mrs. Morgan, you are dismissed," he said.

"Thank you, Your Grace," the cook said, curtsied and gave Gwen a look of apology as she left.

He focused on the maid again, God those eyes. He had to be very careful here. He knew next to nothing about being a Duke, but he did know that one did not dally with the help. Any man who did so was a cad and a scoundrel. A man without honor. One of those unwritten rules, and like the military, in society, unwritten rules were more strictly enforced than the written ones.

Leaning on his cane, he returned to his Grandfather's ... no, it was now his desk.

"Please have a seat, Gwen, this may take a while." Strange, he thought, one did not normally instruct a servant to sit down. Why did he feel uncomfortable sitting while she stood? It was a thought he did not wish to explore. When he reached his chair, he turned and saw that she hadn't moved.

"That was not a request, please sit down."

"Yes sir" she answered and scurried to a seat across the desk.

She gracefully sat. Everything she did was graceful; even that scurry to the chair. Again, why was this woman here?

He studied her. She appeared to be about twenty-one years old. Petit, a few inches over five feet, blond hair that kept trying to escape from her maid's cap. It was the eyes that struck him, bluer, and deeper than any he had ever seen. They reminded him of a high mountain lake on a beautiful summer's day.

Her figure was exceptional, the dress a little tighter than the normal uniform, but it did nothing to distract from her perfect feminine curves. God, get your mind on your duty, focus.

"So Gwen, what happened?" He said calmly, folding his hands and resting them on the desk, determined to remain calm.

Whatever happened it wasn't her fault, in fact, it was more than likely his fault for not being here to solve everything. He mustn't take it out on her he reminded himself, determined to withhold his parade ground voice.

She jumped a little when he asked his question. Her eyes narrowed as she studied him for a second before deciding to go on.

"Sir, the old Duke was sick for a long time," she began hesitantly. "And though I was only a downstairs maid, I think he was not always aware of what was happening. We must be forgiving his problems at the end sir."

My god is she defending the bastard. The old man would be turning over in his grave if he knew that a lowly downstairs maid was sticking up for him. It said something that the only person who'd ever defended the old man was a maid who barely knew him.

"Please go on," Thomas said.

"No one was paid the last quarter before he died sir, and then after he died, and no one came to replace him, no one was paid again. Mr. Evans started telling people they should find employment elsewhere. I know he wrote to someone, but I don't know if he heard anything in return sir." She looked at him, waiting for the explosion

"How long have you been here, on staff I mean?"

"About eight month's sir."

"Do you mean to tell me that you've been working for eight months without being paid?" He demanded.

"Yes, Your Grace," She answered "And Cook and Freddy, I mean Goodwin, also."

"My God! Well, please be assured that everything will be made right."

"Yes Your Grace, I was sure it would be."

What a mess, He wasn't supposed to be the Duke. In fact a few months ago it looked like he wasn't even supposed to be alive. Now here he was, no longer a Major in the King's service, but a Duke of the realm. Responsible for things he didn't even know he was accountable for.

He hadn't been trained for this. That was supposed to be his Uncle John's fate, and after him, Cousin Winslow's served as the spare. But to have the Duke's son John killed by a drunk during a card game on the lower east side. Then to have his older cousin die of the fever all within a month of the old Duke passing, just remarkable.

Being a Duke meant managing vast estates, overseeing the crops, dealing with tenants, attending balls and such. Managing this house, or marrying someone to manage the household. It meant sitting in Parliament and advising the King on important issues of the day.

Dukes were important people doing important things. They were men like the Iron Duke himself. Wellington was what people thought of when picturing a Duke. Not a mere Major, someone without political connections, not someone who'd been trained as a soldier, a damn good one, but still a soldier. What did he know about estates, and agriculture, and pretty maids?

He looked at her again, trying hard to avoid those eyes. Unfortunately, his glance drifted to that shapely figure, and he had to force it back to her face. He settled on her lips, plush and enticing.

"So, you have been keeping house for that entire time?"

"Yes, your Grace, when Mrs. Fischer, Mrs. Evans now I assume, left, she told me that I was the new housekeeper and to keep everything ready for when the new Duke arrived."

"Well, it appears you've done a very good job, please continue, at least until I can figure out how to fix everything. And please prepare my rooms. My bags should be arriving later this afternoon. Have Fre ... I mean Goodwin put them into my room. I'll unpack them myself. And tell Cook that I'll have my meals here in the study for the foreseeable future."

She hesitated, but gathered herself and said, "The accounts at both the butchers and mill are very past due Your Grace. They say they won't send anything more to the main house until the past bills are caught up. They will only talk to the Duke or his secretary. I don't think they trust Mrs. Morgan. She's tried, but they won't extend anymore."

"Yes, of course," he said, surprised that the house didn't do its own butchering. It must have been another of his Grandfather's crazy ideas. A penny short and a pound foolish if you asked him.

"I'll take care of it tomorrow. And, Gwen … what is your last name? If you're to be my housekeeper, I can't keep calling you Gwen, it Miss? …" God let it be Miss and not Mrs. He thought.

"Miss Harding, Your Grace, Gwen Harding," she said, hesitating a little at the last name.

"Well, Miss Harding, thank you for doing such a wonderful job keeping everything together. I'm sure I'll have many more questions for you later. Until then, that should be all for now."

She stood and curtsied, "Very well Your Grace" then turned and left, quietly shutting the door.

He watched her go and marveled. The house had, what? Twelve formal bedrooms? He remembered counting them when he visited one summer. Plus library, dining rooms, parlors, and such, probably twenty-five rooms total.

The house should have a staff of fifteen to twenty people just for the house itself and the kitchen. Then you needed to add the stables, gardeners, and any personal retainers such as valets and ladies maids, it could take more than thirty people to run this place the way it should be run. Truly remarkable, three people thinking they could hold it together.

Thank God for loyal retainers he thought, shaking his head in amazement.

He looked around the room, hoping to spot his Grandfather's account books. This room had always been off limits to him as a boy. He remembered being bored and poking his head in to explore a new room when he was very young. The old bastard had been sitting at this very desk with several account ledgers before him.

An old man even then, he'd spotted the little boy sticking his head round the corner and immediately started yelling that little boys were not to be seen nor heard. Period, end of story. The young Thomas had run away. He hadn't been in this room since.

He found the old leather-bound books and started digging through them. It was going to be a long night, in fact probably a long few nights just to figure out what was what. And in all honesty, it was going to be even harder keeping Miss Harding from intruding into his thoughts.

?

Chapter Two

Gwen woke the next morning, tired and late. She'd spent the night tossing and turning, worried about the future. Things had been going so well. A false sense of hope had started to seep into her. Maybe, just maybe she could put London behind her.

She loved Brookshire and had felt so safe here. Why did everything have to change?

Dressing quickly, Gwen rushed to the kitchen to help Cook prepare breakfast. Running a quick brush through her hair before putting it up under her cap, she thought about the new Duke. She wanted things to go well this morning. It was important that he be happy, it might mean fewer changes. More importantly it might help her stop any more dreams like the ones she'd had last night.

How did he get wounded she wondered, where did he come from, what type of family? All of these thoughts and many more continuously ran through her mind.

No matter what she did, she couldn't stop them. Maybe seeing him again, establishing a routine and the familiarity of his presence would enable her to gain control. Something she so desperately needed to accomplish. She couldn't continue here at Brookshire unless she could control her actions and to some degree those around her.

"Good Morning Mrs. Morgan," Gwen said as she entered the kitchen.

"Good morning my girl, or should I be calling you 'Miss Harding' now that you're the housekeeper for His Grace," she said with a smile from ear to ear.

Gwen was shocked, she hadn't told anyone what His Grace had said the night before. Seeing her confusion, the cook smiled.

"His Grace informed me when I went to clear his dinner things last night," she said. "He said you were to be his housekeeper for now but that he would be sending to the London agencies for more staff. That us three would not need to worry and that our loyalty would be rewarded."

The cook smiled. "And then he said anyone who could keep this place presentable all by herself could probably run a staff of maids and that you'd be the housekeeper."

Gwen was amazed, he'd acted so quickly. A warm glow spread through her as she realized he'd been pleased with her performance. It wasn't just about the security of the position. More about how he saw her, her value and what she'd accomplished.

A warm feeling filled her stomach. He might see her as only a maid, someone "In Service" but he valued her. That was a rather unusual thing for someone in his station in life.

"Did you know the Duke before? I mean before he was the Duke," she asked the cook.

"I knew him for a short while when he was a young one. Used to come for visits during the summer with his mother and father; the old Duke's youngest son. But that stopped when his father died around the time he was eleven or twelve I think."

"What was he like as a little boy?"

"Oh! A holy terror, but in a good way, never mean. Always good with the staff and such. Always into new adventures, used to drive the old Duke crazy. Secretly, I think the old man liked it. The cousins were not very adventurous, mostly kept to themselves and out of the Duke's way."

Turning, Cook removed a pot of water from the stove.

"His Grace, the new one I mean, was never supposed to inherit. There were two sons and a grandson between him and the title. The Old Duke bought him his commission at seventeen, and he was off to follow the drum as they say. That was almost ten years ago."

Gwen thought about what Cook had told her as she made up a breakfast tray and started for the door, then stopped.

"I can't take this to his room," she said, "have you seen Freddy?" she asked in a panic.

"His Grace is in the study, has been all night," answered Cook.

"All night?" Had something been wrong with his room?

He sat behind the large desk, now covered in papers and books. Sometime during the night he'd removed his red uniform tunic and draped it over a chair. He looks tired she thought. His pale face and furrowed brow made her heart ache. His cane rested against the wall behind him.

Standing in the middle of the room with the tray, she waited to be told where he wanted it. After a few moments, The Duke looked up and saw her. Quickly standing, he grabbed his tunic off the chair and put it on.

"By the fire Miss Harding," he said. "I'll get to it in a minute, just need to finish up these figures," he said, staring at the ledgers.

"Yes sir," she said, putting the tray on a table next to a large chair. She knelt and tended the fire placing a log and watching it catch.

She turned and looked at him as he concentrated on his work. He's so handsome, she couldn't think how to explain it, but he was so male, all of the positive things about being a man. His size, quiet confidence, and a physical presence that said he'd seen it all before and could handle anything the world might throw at him.

His wide shoulders tapered down to narrow hips. His hair was cut short in the military style. She wondered what it would look like long and hanging to his shoulders. She stood there for several minutes watching.

He continued his work. Looking up, he was surprised to find her still there. He raised an eyebrow, "is there anything else?" He asked.

Embarrassed at getting caught. She stood up straight.

"Cook said I was not to leave until I saw you eating Your Grace," she said. A little lie, enough to give her some cover. She watched his eyes to see if he'd get mad, looking for any signs of a pending explosion. She wasn't surprised when he didn't over react. He might be loud and commanding at times, but always in control of himself.

 She was surprised however when he smiled. It transformed his face, making him look younger and a little more approachable. She breathed a short sigh.

"She did, did she? Well then, I guess I'll take my break now. She's probably worried about her food getting cold."

He walked to the large chair next to the table, leaning on his stick. He caught her looking at it, hesitated a moment, then shrugged and continued on.

"I should have eaten in the dining room, probably would have been easier on everyone," he said as he raised the doomed silver serving dish. His brow rose in surprise at the plate of fried eggs, and four large slices of toast liberally smeared with raspberry jam.

"It appears I'll have to take care of the butcher situation today, A man can't continue to have breakfast without meat, preferably several different types," he said to no one in particular.

She saw that he was smiling and realized he wasn't critical, just making conversation.

"Yes sir, and now that I see you are truly breaking your fast, I can safely return to the kitchen and report to Cook." She smiled and gave a quick curtsy before turning and walking to the door.

She could feel his eyes following her all the way across the room and out the door. Once safely on the other side, she leaned back against the oaken door and sighed. Get hold of yourself Gwen. He's just a man and we all know what they're like.

.oOo.

Gwen joined Cook in a light breakfast and then scurried upstairs to His Grace's bedroom to make sure everything was acceptable. Knowing the Duke was still in the study, Gwen assured herself that it would be safe. Entering the room, she saw that he truly had spent the night working. The big master bed had not been slept in.

An old beaten leather trunk sat in the middle of the room where Freddy had left it the afternoon before. She felt a strong urge to peek inside and learn more about the man. Looking over her shoulder at the empty doorway, Gwen knelt down and undid the buckles and slowly raised the huge upper half.

A warm, manly smell of wood smoke and soft pine needles greeted her. The trunk was filled with red uniforms and a set of evening, dress clothes. She ran her hands over the fabric, imagining where they'd been. What battles had they seen? Briefly closing her eyes, she imagined him marching across a field, leading his men into battle.

It couldn't have all been battles and blood. There must have been good times too. Oh, how he must have looked dancing at an embassy balls.

She closed her eyes again and heard the soft music, could see him dancing the waltz with a beautiful Parisian lady. Maybe someone who'd lost her husband in the war. A charming brunet, looking at the British Major with bedroom eyes. A spurt of jealousy flashed through Gwen, and she laughed at herself, these flights of fancy had a way of getting away from her.

Deciding that His Grace would not be upset, she started hanging up the clothes. It bothered her to see them folded up in the trunk.

At the bottom, she found a small wooden box. Placing it on top of his dresser, she glanced over her shoulder again at the empty bedroom door. Lifting the lid she saw two gold cufflinks, a diamond stick pin, and four gold medals attached to colorful ribbons. Hesitating a moment, she lifted out each one, examining the engravings, fingering the ribbon. Trying to imagine what he'd done to win them.

An overwhelming desire to know everything about him rushed through her and settled in the bottom of her stomach. A sense of sadness followed the feeling. She would never be allowed to know. She had no right to wonder even.

Realizing how silly she was being, she gently placed the last medal back in the box and gently closed the lid.

"Miss Harding?" A strong male voice called from the door.

Gwen about jumped out of her skin and quickly turned to see the subject of her thoughts standing there like a giant oak tree, his eyebrows as high as eyebrows ever got.

"Can I help you with something?" he asked.

She was truly and surely caught. Why do things like this always happen to her?

"I'm sorry Your Grace, I thought to put your clothes away and noticed the box and the medals. I'm sorry, but my curiosity got the better of me. It won't happen again," she said, looking at the ground in shame.

The Duke was silent for a long moment and then said, "Thank you, I wasn't looking forward to the chore. My man will be here in a few days to take care of these types of things. My batman, Corporal Reynolds will be my valet."

Sneaking a look she saw that he didn't appear to be angry. Gwen breathed a silent sigh of relief and clasped the side of her dress to stop her hands from shaking. It had been a close thing. Something she promised herself that would never happen again. She wouldn't cross into the Duke's bedroom ever again she swore.

"Yes sir, will the rest of your things be arriving with him?" She asked, hoping to change the subject.

"This is all of my things," he said, nodding to the trunk. "Quite a lot to show for nine years, don't you think?" A look of slight sadness crossed his eyes for a brief second and then he looked off into the distance remembering those years.

It's more than I have to show for twenty one years she thought to herself.

"Yes sir, and again I am sorry," she said, starting for the door and a quick escape. But he didn't move. Leaning on his cane, he filled the doorway, blocking her way out. Her heart skipped a beat, what does he want?

The man looked down at her from his towering height, his eyes guarded as he considered something. He looked at the bed for a moment and then back at her. His eyes lost in unknowable thoughts.

Finally making up his mind, he stepped back to let her pass. Gwen felt a hot flush fill her body as she scooted past the man. What was it about him that made her get flustered like this? Her heart raced as she hurried down the hall, having to fight not to break into a run.

.oOo.

Later that evening she wanted to have Freddy take the Duke his dinner but, of course, the boy couldn't be found when he was most needed. Reluctantly she brought the dinner tray into the study and felt herself flush with embarrassment when she thought about the scene in his bedroom earlier in the day.

The Duke sat behind his huge desk looking at several maps. His brows scrunched in thought. He reminded her of a General getting ready for battle. Without looking up, he absently nodded to the table by the fire

Gwen quickly placed the tray on the table and turned to leave when the Duke said, "Thank you, Miss Harding." His smile had returned; it could melt one of Cook's cast iron pans. "A friend of mine should be arriving tomorrow or the day after," he said. "Sergeant Major Bowen," he added.

Is this to be the new butler she wondered? It was obvious that Brookshire should have a butler, preferably of the regal, austere variety. Someone to intimidate both the staff and any visitors. Why couldn't things stay the way they were. Where do you place a Sergeant Major was her next thought, is he to be in the servants quarters.

His Grace had said 'Friend' so not servant's quarters.

As if reading her mind he said, "Please make up a room in the east wing. While this will be his permanent home, he'll be traveling a lot. I want him to be comfortable coming and going."

So not a butler then? "Have you known him long, sir?" She said, immediately regretting it, her nosiness getting away from her again.

"He was my corporal in my first platoon when I was commissioned a new Ensign. We served together ever since. More years have passed by than I want to think about. But yes, I have known him a long time. Too long and too much history," he mumbled to himself. "A better man you'll never meet," he added.

"I will take care of everything, and we will ensure he knows that he is welcome at Brookshire."

"Thank you, Miss Harding, I knew you would take care of things."

She left the room sighing. It seemed that the earlier incident had been put behind them. Now if only she could get through the night without disturbing dreams.

The   Reluctant   Duke

.

Made in the USA
Coppell, TX
03 June 2021